YOU CAN'T CATCH ME

Somewhat against his better judgment, Mike Wells accepts a lucrative assignment from bigtime gangster Rico Bruck. It seems a simple enough job: to board a train and shadow a man on his journey to New York, and then to telephone his whereabouts to Bruck. Mike takes with him the beautiful Toni Kaye, who tells him she wants to escape Bruck's employment and make a career as a singer. But when they arrive at their destination, their target is found murdered . . .

LAWRENCE LARIAR

YOU CAN'T CATCH ME

Complete and Unabridged

LINFORD
Leicester

First published in Great Britain

First Linford Edition
published 2019

A catalogue record for this book is available
from the British Library.

ISBN 978–1–4448–4171–8

Published by
F. A. Thorpe (Publishing)
Anstey, Leicestershire

Set by Words & Graphics Ltd.
Anstey, Leicestershire
Printed and bound in Great Britain by
T. J. International Ltd., Padstow, Cornwall

This book is printed on acid-free paper

1

I wheeled my crate through the entrance to the Card Club, a stone-and-metal gateway that bore only the simple legend RICO BRUCK on the high edge of the masonry. It was a simple sign, a copper square as dignified as the front door to a ladies' seminary. The pebbled drive led up to a long, low and rambling building, rigged to look like a millionaire's hideaway among the big oaks on the smooth lawns that lined the lake.

I parked my car in the quiet circle on the north side of the house. I pulled out my little sketch pad and started a drawing of the doorman. There was time to waste. My date with Rico was a good half-hour away.

So I sketched the big ape. He stood with his feet planted before the door, his hands locked behind his back, as he rolled and rocked on his heels. He was dressed in a doorman's costume, something out of the court of Louis the Fourteenth maybe, complete with gold braid and enough buttons to start a factory. He looked big and strong and dignified. All but his face.

I sketched the broad, flat plane of his jaw. He had a face straight out of the crime books; a menacing mug calculated to make all visitors pause and reflect before entering Rico Bruck's sanctum without an invitation. He had a broken nose, fat and square. Somebody had hit him head-on, long ago. Somebody had tagged him forever with the pulpy proboscis of the seasoned pug, the mushed and mangled mark of the professional thug. His face was easy to put down on paper, even for me, an amateur caricaturist. Once I would have sketched this head in detail, giving it the full treatment with the soft pencils and the rubbed shadows. But my zeal for an art career had died a long time ago, before I entered the army. Now I only doodled my pictures, putting down

2

interesting faces for my file wherever I found them. Over the years, I had sketched them all, in police line-ups and court-rooms. Some people collect stamps or old china or cigar bands. I collected faces. I finished the profile shot of the gorilla and folded it away. It was time to see Rico Bruck now.

At the door, the ape held up a hand. He opened his mouth and the flicker of his dentures showed plenty of gold in his flabby mouth.

'I saw you making a picture,' he growled.

'You saw right,' I said.

'Tear it up.'

'What the hell are you — an art critic, or a doorman?' I asked. Up close, he was as tall as I, but stacked for moving girders, broad and beefy around the shoulders.

'Rico don't like people to make pictures without he gives them permission,' said the monster. 'So tear it up like a good boy.'

He had his giant paw held out, palm up, as casual as a collector of tickets in a theater lobby. He showed me the hard edge of his scowl and took one step my way. I didn't budge. He continued to move his hand toward my arm, so that I had to slap it down to promote my strength of character. He paused in his purpose to appraise me carefully, making up his mind about me and finding me a problem.

I said, 'Why not let Rico decide about my work of art?'

'You want Rico?' he asked.

'I've got a date with Rico.'

'Later,' he said, eyeing me with the wide-open stare of the punchy fighter, as shallow as the depth of his intellect. 'Come back when the place is open.'

'It's open now. Rico wants me.'

'Who? Rico wants who?'

'Me. Mike Wells.'

'You got a card, chum?'

'A date,' I said. 'I have a date, not a card.'

'What for? You selling something?'

'Pistachio nuts. Rico wants to buy my pretty pistachio nuts.'

'*Nuts* is what I say,' said the ape,

4

shaking his head stubbornly and closing his eyes. He rocked back and forth, a tempting target if I could catch him on the backswing. 'If Rico asks you to come here, he gives you a card, see? You show me the card or roll the hell out of here. Orders is orders.'

He was giving me the business, the routine check that all strangers must undergo before passing through the front portals into the exclusive interior of the Card Club. I had heard about the procedure, a legendary rule created to ensure an exclusive attendance inside the mansion. Rico Bruck catered only to the upper-class gambling maniacs in Chicago, the deluxe trade he drew from the socially elite, the famous, the infamous, and the notorious characters who patronized his gaming tables. It was a system he had inaugurated three years ago, a successful gimmick that eliminated the middle-class enthusiasts, and thus restricted his wheels of chance to the fancier folk who could afford to lose their loot and go away smiling, to return another day. A small black card admitted the regulars into the ornate dining hall, where they were treated to a gourmet's feast, for free, before passing on to the dice and roulette.

I said, 'Use your head, big boy, Rico's going to be mad at you if I leave this dump.'

'Orders is orders.'

His stupidity goosed me into anger and I sidestepped him toward the door. In that moment, his larded hand reached out for me and grabbed me up high on the shoulder. He was a big bad boy and he had a grip that lifted my jacket and held it as gently as a bulldozer playing with a tree stump. He jerked me back and off-balance, but I gave him my elbow as I fell his way and he grunted and released the pressure on my shoulder. After that, we were all over each other. I had figured him for an ex-pug, the type of strong man who goes soft in the navel as time eats the hardness out of the muscles. I figured him wrong.

He must have been a professional wrestler in his youth. He tripped me neatly, and on the way down his big fist caught me near the gut, hard enough to make me pause and think my way out of his next attack. I let him come to me, and when his great head leaned my way, I kicked up at his groin and caught him under the belt line with my knee. He gasped and grunted and called me a dirty name. But he was falling now.

We rolled off the thin strip of concrete and down on the graveled driveway. We kicked up a lot of dust and pebbles and I worked him around for a quick stab at his sweating face. He was grinning down at me, enjoying the exercise, his pig eyes burning with a happy gleam. He missed me with his left, his iron fist skimming past my ear and smacking the pebbled drive. He recoiled in pain, and in that quick tick of torment I decided to put him away. I kicked up at him and this time my toe found its mark. He sagged and grabbed for his stomach, his eyes closed against the pain. I crossed a right to his jaw and he dropped away and hit the curbing with a flat slap. I was angry enough to dish out more, but the sound of a car rolling up the driveway changed my mind.

There was a girl in the car, and she was

screaming 'Elmo!' in a high and hysterical voice. She parked the car a few inches from his head and hopped out. She was something special, a trim blonde with a smooth and stimulating stride. She kneeled to examine me, allowing me to sample the close-up of her bumps and hollows, skillfully displayed and accented by the simple silk ensemble she wore. She had a warm and husky voice, as provocative as an amateur Tallulah Bankhead.

'Did he hurt you?' she asked.

'I'll live,' I said, getting off my butt and brushing the pebbles away. The doorman blinked his eyes, and when he saw her his face went dumb and simpering, like a schoolboy caught in the pickle jar.

'What's it all about, Elmo?' she asked.

'This jerk said he wanted in,' Elmo said. 'But he don't show me no card . . . So I ask him — '

'And I told him,' I interrupted. 'Shall I tell you now?'

'Tell me,' she said pleasantly.

'My name is Mike Wells, and Rico sent for me.'

'Well now, Mike,' she said. She had

8

been staring at me curiously, but when I mouthed my name, her attitude changed and her smile broadened and she slipped into easy laughter — not mean, not nasty, but as friendly as a warm handshake. Her laugh had the same quality as her husky dialogue, and a little more. She showed her amusement in a relaxed way, so that you thought immediately how nice it would be if you could get her to listen privately to a few of your real belly laughs. 'I owe you an apology.'

'You owe him what?' the ape asked.

'I'm sorry,' she continued, disregarding the big doorman. 'It's my fault, Mike. I should have told Elmo here that Mr. Bruck was expecting you. Mr. Bruck told me last night that he was expecting a man out to see him. But I guess I got here too late to tell Elmo.'

'You see, Elmo?' I asked.

'Nuts!' said Elmo.

'Follow me, Mike,' the girl said.

So I followed her. She led me into a broad foyer, decorated with an expert's eye for authentic detail. The place was lush, an intimate room festooned with furniture and fixtures right out of the antique shops. It was tough to appraise the decor, because the girl ahead of me walked with a movement calculated to turn a man's bones to marrow. She had good hips and knew what to do with them. Her long-legged stride was aimed at a small hat-check booth under the delicately curved stairway. Here, she paused.

'Ever been here before, Mike?' she asked.

I was examining a tapestry draped on the wall near the stairway, a priceless slice of material featuring a galloping centaur pursuing a naked sprite through the ferns.

'He's gaining on her,' I said.

'He'll never grab her.' She smiled. 'We have all kinds of art inside in the big room.'

'I've heard about it.'

'Too bad it's locked now. Otherwise I could take you in on the dollar tour.'

She bent to phone Rico, after which she invited me to pull up a chair.

'Mr. Bruck is going to be busy for a while. You don't mind waiting, I hope?'

'I had a date with him,' I said. 'What's holding him up?'

'It must be Mr. Gilligan, I guess. Every Wednesday, Mr. Gilligan and Mr. Bruck sort of have a business conference. Mr. Gilligan is the lawyer for this place.'

'The place needs a lawyer?' I asked. I knew the answer, but she was helping me kill time, a pleasant doll who was easy to stay with for more reasons than one. She ran through a quick breakdown of John Gilligan for me, describing him accurately and laying on heavily with the respect for his legalistic powers. I watched her mouth move, fascinated by the seductive curve of her lips, a showgirl's smile that was automatic, but as provocative as a warm bath. She wound up her description and said, 'Listen, maybe you'd like a drink of something?'

'Try me with some Scotch.'

She tried me. She came out from behind the booth and walked to a small bar at the far end of the lobby, then returned with the best brand and a glass and a mixer and some ice. She poured me a generous taste of it.

'Who do I thank for the stuff?' I asked.

'You can call me Toni.'

'One of the twins?'

'Just Toni,' she said. 'Toni Kaye.'

She was friendly and warm enough to share the Scotch with me, sipping an occasional swallow while casing the doorway at the foot of the stairs.

'Rico Bruck doesn't like the help to indulge,' she said.

'For you he should make special rules, Toni.'

'It's house policy,' she said seriously. 'I've been here too long to start breaking rules.'

'You're wasting your time in a trap like this,' I commented. 'What's the future for a babe like you?'

'You're nice, Mike. Sometimes I get sore at Rico for the way this place is run — so strict, I mean. But he gets a lot of fancy people in here all the time. And help is help, so we have to stay where we belong.' She frowned a minute. 'That's one of the reasons why I'm hoping to get out of here soon.'

'Don't tell me Rico won't let you mix

with the rich lads who waltz in here?'

'Maybe I don't go for those rich lads.'

'What do you go for?'

'I've got simple tastes,' she said.

'How simple must I get?' I asked.

She laughed it up and took another swallow from my glass. She was enjoying my company and making no bones about showing her goodwill. She leaned over the counter in her niche, and it wasn't easy to concentrate on her face. And around her the smell of a tantalizing perfume hung in the air and worked at my sensibilities. She became communicative about her ambitions as a singer, and I told her frankly that she could make the grade. Even without a voice.

'You're kidding me about my voice,' she said. 'But I'm serious, Mike. I've been wanting to sing professionally for ages.'

'Let's have a sample.'

'Oh, not here. Not now. But one of these days I'm going to tear myself loose from this place and make a try at a singing career.'

'What will Rico say to that?'

'Say?' Her eyebrows arched and for the

first time she showed me another facet of her emotional set-up. She registered scorn and disdain for Rico Bruck and his palatial loot trap. 'Listen, can't I get a job like this anywhere?'

'As a hat-check wren? But of course.'

'That's what I mean. You see, what I want is a chance at New York, the big time. From what I've heard, you don't need much to get this kind of a job there. One of these days I'm going to make the switch. You know anybody in New York?'

'I have a branch office there.'

'Show people, I mean.'

'Some of my best friends, baby.'

'You're kidding me.'

'Am I? Ever heard of Lawrence Keddy?'

'Lawrence Keddy, the agent?' she gushed. 'That's like asking whether I heard of Harry Truman.' She was excited now, her long and delicate hand touching mine in a gesture of friendliness, as natural as her smile. 'How well do you know him?'

'He's a pal of mine.'

'Can you get him to listen to me?'

'I can get him to take you on,' I said. 'If you can sing half as well as you can smile.'

She was on fire for me when the phone buzzed and interrupted our chitchat. She answered the ring politely and told Rico Bruck that I was on my way inside. But her free hand did not lift away from mine, telegraphing her reluctance to see me leave.

I stayed. 'Rico may want me to go to New York for him,' I said.

She laughed, still clutching my hand. 'You'd better go upstairs now. Rico doesn't like to be kept waiting.'

'If I go to New York, I may leave right away.'

'Meaning what?'

'Can't you guess?' I asked. 'I'm trying to promote free transportation for you.'

'Maybe I'd rather pay my own freight.'

'We can discuss it later,' I said.

She shook her head at me laughingly. 'You certainly can sell, Mike.'

'When do you go off?'

'I'm free at about two in the morning.'

'And where do you go?'

'Home,' she said. 'Where all good girls go after work.'

'Good boys visit good girls,' I suggested. 'If good boys know the right address.'

'You're twisting my arm,' Toni said. 'I'll see you on the way out, Mike.'

'Try and avoid me,' I said, and left it at that.

2

There was a stout mahogany door beyond the stairs, on which a gold plate carried the name *Rico Bruck* etched in classic italics. I knocked discreetly, and from somewhere inside a voice shouted, 'Okay, Wells,' and then I pushed the door open and walked in.

It was a tremendous room, decorated in a more businesslike motif, with smooth and polished paneling and the modest overtones of a tycoon's private chamber. Rico got up from behind his king-sized desk and greeted me with warmth and a high-pressure handshake.

He introduced me to his legal brain, John Gilligan, tall and lean and with a courtroom smile as phony as his uppers. 'This,' said Rico, 'is Mike Wells. Probably the best private dick in the business, John.'

17

'I've heard the name,' said Gilligan with a polite smile.

'You did a big job on the Lippy Maggee case, didn't you?'

'I helped a little.'

'Oh, you did better than that,' Gilligan said. He waved his hand at an invisible fly, then put his hands in his pockets and rocked and rolled on his heels in an attitude reminiscent of the ape doorman. 'I attended parts of that trial, and it seemed to me that it was your evidence that helped convict Maggee.'

'He's modest,' Rico said. 'That's what I like about him. How many private dicks you know who don't jump in and grab all the credit? Mike, now, he's different. He knows his stuff and he does his stuff, and no fancy talk and crapping around.' He paused to wink his slow wink at Gilligan. 'He'll probably get a big charge out of the crummy thing we're about to hand him.'

Rico Bruck had the facility for projecting intimacy and an attitude of friendliness where none existed. It was part of the legend of his success in the hierarchy of crime, this phony camaraderie he could turn on with such conviction. He was a dapper character, small and slim, who carried himself with the cool poise of a successful businessman. He would have looked at home behind the manager's desk in a department store, or at the helm of any enterprise involving personality and executive know-how. He had a sharp, eager face, long-nosed and hard in the cheeks and jowls. But it was his eyes that carried the weight of his temperament. They were blue and brilliant, the optics of the creative ruler of empire, the eyes of authority and intellect.

He broke out a bottle and insisted that we drink and talk nonsense for a while. He had the manners of a gentleman. You drank his liquor and listened to his oiled repartee and forgot that this was the man who had come up through the ranks of thugs and gunmen of the bootleg era to establish himself as the czar of all the racketeers in the Middle West. Rico Bruck moved among the city greats, the officials and celebrities and society bigwigs, but his source of income still came from the backwash areas of the world of almost-legalized crime: the numbers game and the bookie business and his famous Card Club.

John Gilligan rested his bony frame in an easy chair and conducted the conversation with his expected courtroom flair for managing dialogue. At ease near the window, he looked for all the world like a British peer on the loose for a fast cup of tea and a few scones. He sipped his drink in delicate pauses. He fingered his thread of a mustache with finesse. His saturnine face remained deadpan as he mouthed his well-constructed sentences. But he handled his job with aplomb, subtly guiding the tête-à-tête into channels in which I was involved, so that soon we were engaged in a talk about my business alone. And after that, it was a short jump to the problem at hand.

'Rico's insisted that you're the man for this job, Wells,' Gilligan said. 'And after talking to you, I'm inclined to agree with him. Your chore involves discretion and sound, independent judgment. I think you're well equipped to handle it.'

'I haven't said I'd take it yet,' I reminded him.

Rico burst into unfeigned merriment.

'See what I mean, John?' he roared. 'This is not a man you can con into a deal. He's cagey, as smart as you are.'

'I don't doubt it for a minute.' Gilligan smiled. He put down his glass and produced a pipe, lit it slowly and deliberately, then leaned on his bony knees and grinned at me. 'But I know Wells can't turn down this deal, because it's so damnably simple and yet pays so well. I'm sure Wells is interested in an easy buck, as the saying goes?'

'Start with the dough,' I suggested. 'The job can come later.'

'You'll be paid a grand for the deal,' said Rico. 'Is that sugar?'

'Not sugar, Rico. A grand for a private investigator can be too much for too little. Maybe you want somebody else, because I only play the legal jobs.'

Rico opened his mouth to talk, but John Gilligan waved him into silence. Rico caught the signal and relaxed behind his desk, rolling a yellow pencil in his little hand and watching his legal advisor for the next part of the byplay.

'This job is strictly legal, of course,'

said Gilligan, as calm as a dead herring and just as emotional. 'Rico is interested in a character who leaves tomorrow night on the Century, for New York. This man is a sitting duck for you, Wells. He will probably become one of the simplest assignments you've ever had. In the first place, he is ponderously fat. He is so fat that it would be impossible for him to hide from you, to lose himself in a crowd.'

'You want him tailed?'

'Exactly. Rico merely wants to know where this fat man goes when he arrives in New York.'

'You spot him, that's all,' Rico said.

'One day's work for a thousand dollars,' said Gilligan.

'That's a lot of loot for a small job.'

'It's worth it to me,' said Rico. He rolled his eyes in a quick exchange with Gilligan. 'I'll get it back, Wells.'

'I wasn't worried about that angle,' I said. 'But why me for the job?'

'I like you.'

'And I love you dearly, Rico. But still, why me?'

'Questions,' said Rico to Gilligan. 'You

see what I meant, John? This boy's got something upstairs. He's brainy.'

'Flattery will get you nowhere,' I insisted. 'You've got a whole squad of gunsels who could track a rat through the sewers of Times Square and come back with a mink pelt. You've got plenty of willing little workers, Rico, busy bees who can knock off a thing like this with no effort at all.'

'I have?' Rico asked his ashtray. 'Maybe you can name me one, Wells?'

'I don't pal around with your lads.'

'I don't blame you,' Gilligan said quietly. 'Rico is right, my friend. His staff of assistants are a notch above the grade of moron, actually.'

'Not only that,' Rico added. 'It isn't because they're all so damned dumb, Wells. Point is, this fat character is smart, you understand? Do you send a boy out on a man's job? And suppose the fat boy knows a couple of my men, what then? A man running, he feels a hell of a lot better if he knows who's chasing him, right? And if he knows they're after him — why, he really makes tracks. He really fades.'

'The fat man is tricky,' Gilligan said. 'He's smart enough to smell out any of Rico's boys. That's why we need a man like you, Wells. You can't pass up a jaunt like this. Rico will pay all your expenses, deluxe style, including a drawing room on the Century, plus the best suite in my hotel, the Brentworth. Compliments of the management, of course.'

It was a caviar-and-canápes assignment. It was steak and onions, money in the bank, a gold brick on a plate for any private investigator in his right mind. But I checked my growing enthusiasm, despite the fact that the journey might include Toni Kaye as roommate on the Century. Their uninhibited zeal and the ardor of their pitch goosed my natural caution.

John Gilligan was bending every effort to sell me the trip. His presence in this room was calculated to lend dignity and decorum to the pitch. He was oily and smooth, an expensive huckster for so simple a deal. Why was he knocking himself out? They were hard at work promoting something that looked ripe for an intelligent high-school lad with a mail-order detective's badge. My record and my background rose up to challenge their honeyed words. Any detective worthy of his fodder looks twice at an offer coming from such a man as Rico Bruck. He could be using me for a tool, a stooge, an outside handyman on a mission involving illegal hijinks. I let the silence build, watching them carefully in the pause. They gave me nothing but dead-pan quiet, patiently awaiting my decision.

I said, 'Tell me more, Rico.'

'More of what?'

'The pitch.'

'You know the pitch,' Rico said, turning to Gilligan for moral support. 'We leave out anything, John?'

Gilligan rested his regal neck against the back of the chair. He puffed slowly on his Dunhill. He opened his eyes and stared at the burst of smoke. 'Not a thing, Wells. You know all there is to know, my friend.'

'Everything,' said Rico.

I plucked my hat off my knee. I put it on my head and stood up and started for the door, watching them freeze as I moved away.

'Good day, gents,' I said. 'It's been a lovely little party.'

'I say, now,' said Gilligan, back on his feet again. 'What's eating you, Wells?'

'Maybe I don't go for legal doubletalk, Gilligan.'

'Legal? I don't understand what you're getting at.'

'You lawyers have one-way tracks of understanding,' I said quietly. 'What do you need, a fancy writ before you start laying the facts on the line? You've talked me around the old garden gate, Gilligan, but you haven't said much of any interest to a detective. Maybe you'd better start all over again.'

'Relax, Wells,' Rico said, taking my arm as gently as a Boy Scout leading an old lady across a busy street. 'You got a bad temper. What's bothering you?'

'The fat boy,' I said. 'Who is he?'

'You'll see him tomorrow,' said Gilligan. 'I'll point him out to you in the station.'

'Doubletalk again. Who is he?'

Silence. And then the quick exchange of wide-open amazement at my question. Gilligan put down his pipe and struck a pose calculated to convince me of his intrinsic honesty, the type of stance he might use on a fickle jury, complete with boyish innocence ripe on his bony face.

'Will you believe me if I tell you we don't know his name?'

'Frankly, no.'

'It's true,' said Rico anxiously. 'So help me, Wells, it's true.'

'Let me put it this way,' Gilligan said, putting it the way he chose with a well-oiled gesture of his outstretched hand, palm down and designed to quiet me. He kept his hand that way as he talked, half-closing his eyes and making heavy and ponderous furrows in his brow as he expounded his case. 'There are certain situations in which a man like Rico can become involved that lie outside the province of the usual. What I mean is, this assignment may sound rather odd to you, Wells. But in the final judgment, you must rely on the character of your client when making a decision. What Rico is asking you to do is only a normal procedure in your line of business. He wants a man followed to New York. You've done the same chore on many occasions before this. You must consider this job just as routine as any of the others you've handled.'

He was good. He was great. But he didn't reckon with my natural apathy toward all members of the bar. There wasn't a lawyer on earth I could ever learn to love. In my book they were mental maggots, the leeches who sucked blood and lived off misery and corruption. Unless you needed one . . .

I said, 'A great speech, Gilligan. Wonderful. But here's another small question for you to chew on. Why do you want this fat slug tailed?'

Gilligan exchanged a sly smile with Rico, slow and easy, the way two parents might react to a foolish question from a growing boy. 'There are certain things we can't tell you about the fat man, of course,' Gilligan said easily. 'You must have had jobs like this before, Wells — cases where the client only gives the orders without revealing the background for the chase?'

'I've had them,' I said. 'But this is my first for Rico Bruck.'

They caught the impact of my line. I

saw Rico's eyes flick to Gilligan, a second's slide, but enough to quiet the tall man. Then Rico came my way and stood over me, small and weak-looking even up close. His face, however, was set and grim, as tight as the hard line of his jutting jaw. He reached into his jacket, pulled out his wallet and began to drop bills in my lap — fifties — slowly enough for me to count them as they fell, twenty of them. He paused when the last one fluttered to rest. He continued to count, ten more bills; five hundred extra.

'Fifteen hundred bucks,' said Rico, barely raising his voice. 'And you get an extra five hundred when I come to New York and you tell me where I can lay my hands on the fat slob.'

'He must be worth his weight in gold,' I observed.

'The fat man is loaded,' Rico said.

'With what?'

'You get your dough for what we explained, and no questions.'

I stacked the green stuff into a neat bundle. I placed the bundle on Rico's desk.

'Stuff it,' I said.

The little man reacted with a fine display of temper. His pale cheeks flooded with crimson and he opened his mouth and spluttered an obscenity at me. But Gilligan stepped between us in time to save me from boiling over.

'Take it easy, boys,' he said, still the calm and legal arbiter. 'No need to get your dander up, Wells. You can't blame Rico for wanting to keep the lid on this deal. Look at it this way; it's perfectly legal, but it involves a man who is not considered *pure* in police circles. I'm talking about Monk Stang, of course.'

He dropped the name quietly, but Rico spat violently into a convenient cuspidor at the mention of Monk Stang. He had spat before, and he would spit again, because Monk and he were arch-enemies in the world of criminal endeavor. For the past five years Monk Stang had been slowly insinuating himself into the Chicago rackets, a procedure that had resulted in inter-mob friction on several occasions. In the dim and distant years, during Prohibition and later, Monk and

Rico had been partners, henchmen, conspirators in assorted larceny and mayhem. But Rico graduated to the more refined rackets in the forties, deserting his partner in New York. After that the breach widened. And when Monk arrived in Chicago all hell broke loose, especially in the neighborhoods dominated by Rico's gambling establishments. There had been a truce between them last year. Something must have happened to open the rift and renew the ancient feud. I took a stab at guessing.

'The Folsom pendant?' I asked. 'Is that what the fat boy has?'

'You see how smart he is?' Rico said. 'He guesses good.'

'How could I miss?'

Gilligan smiled feebly at Rico. 'Let's lay it on the line for Wells, Rico. He's not stupid, after all. Everybody in Chicago knows that you were down at police headquarters after the Folsom pendant was stolen last week. It requires no great deductive powers to add two and two. Since Monk Stang appeared down there at the same time you did, the assumption is that either of you might have been involved in the theft of that pendant.'

He continued his monologue, breaking down the Folsom case with a fine regard for detail. Everybody who reads the Sunday supplements is aware of the fabulous history of the Folsom pendant, a bauble that has long fascinated the public because of its historical background. It is reputed to be the creation of Cargini, who had designed it for the Czar of all the Russias before the Revolution. It is a magnificent cluster of priceless gems surrounding a giant stone almost as large as the Hope diamond and valued at over half a million. The treasure had been lifted from the Chicago home of Everett Folsom, despite the usual precautions. The heist was a masterpiece of burglary.

The police grabbed Monk Stang first because of his reputation for this type of thievery; Monk was the master strategist in chores of this sort. But Monk escaped with an airtight alibi, and so did Rico Bruck. Their session in the D.A.'s office was strictly routine, but there had been hard and violent exchanges between them, enough to make the headlines for a day or two. For my dough, only Monk Stang could have engineered the job. The Folsom pendant was a challenge for his talents.

I waited for Gilligan to unwind himself, spouting another five minutes of legal doubletalk calculated to put my mind at rest permanently.

'Let's say that Rico suspects the fat man of carrying the Folsom pendant to New York for Monk Stang,' said Gilligan. 'All we want you to do is follow him discreetly.'

'Why should Fatso be heading for New York?' I asked. 'There are plenty of cooperative fences here in Chicago.'

'A good question,' said Rico. 'Tell him, Johnny.'

'Monk Stang is in New York,' Gilligan said.

'And you want the fat boy before he reaches Monk?'

'That's a pretty sound theory.'

'You two will be in New York?'

'We're taking a plane tonight,' Rico said. 'We'll be there a long time ahead of you, at the Waldorf. You got a snap job, Wells. You just follow the fat man until he settles down. When that happens, you let me know. What have you got to lose? You doing anything wrong, tailing a man for a customer?' He picked up the stack of bills and held them out to me. 'Don't be a dope, Wells. Take the bundle.'

I took it. 'When do I leave?'

'I've reserved a drawing room for you,' Gilligan smiled. 'I'll meet you at Union Station this afternoon at five-thirty, to point out your quarry.'

3

Toni Kaye was waiting for me in the driveway when I came out, chatting idly with the ape in the monkey suit. I tugged her away and strolled toward my car.

'You'd better pack your duds,' I told her. 'We're leaving for New York tonight.'

'We?' she laughed. 'You throw a fast pitch, Mike.'

'Why waste time?'

'Sometimes it's better slow and easy.'

'That's for the birds, Toni.' I piloted her into my car, sat her down and gave her a cigarette. She closed her eyes and blew smoke and meditated. She threw her head back and stretched with animal movements. Her blonde hair was as natural as the green leaves above us. She sucked casually at the cigarette. She crossed her legs and I saw that her well-molded knees

35

were unstockinged. I said, 'I haven't got time for games because the train pulls out in a couple of hours.'

'Give a gal a minute to make up her mind, Mike.'

'What's your problem?'

'The job at Rico's earns me good money.'

'You'll do all right,' I said. 'You can always do as well as Rico's in New York.'

'And suppose I miss?'

'I'll be there.'

'You'll stay there?'

'I can be sold the idea,' I said, and dropped my hand over her shoulder. 'I have a branch office in New York.'

She opened her eyes and turned her body so that she could appraise me. There was a budding curiosity moving her eyebrows, an expression that told me she was capable of deep and penetrating thought. 'A branch office?' she asked. 'What's your line?'

'I'm a private investigator.'

'And you're working *for* Rico?'

Was it fear that clouded her eyes? She stared out over the lake, moving her body away from me. A plane hummed high in the western sky but she was looking somewhere beyond it, deeper into the blue and through the blue and out of this world, into her own personal landscape. What she saw there didn't charm her.

'What's wrong with working for Rico?' I asked.

'I didn't say it was wrong. What are you doing for him?'

I patted her hand. 'A private eye doesn't divulge his client's little secrets, baby.'

'I'm sorry,' she said absently. 'I didn't know. But maybe I better stay where I am for the time being, Mike.'

'You worried about what I'm doing?'

'Maybe I'm just worried about myself.'

'That's crazy, baby. What I'm doing for Rico shouldn't bother you.'

'I don't want to get mixed up in anything with Rico.'

'You won't come near it.'

'I don't want it.' She seemed to shiver a bit, pulling her arms close to her sides as though a cold wind had swept over her. 'That's another reason why I want to get away from here.'

'Rico bothers you?'

'Not yet, he doesn't.'

'You're expecting it?'

She closed her eyes and flipped her cigarette away. Her lips were brilliant scarlet, the make-up of the seasoned theatrical gal, skillfully blended to complement her darkish skin color. She frowned thoughtfully at some secret problem. She was wearing a powerful and penetrating fragrance, a perfume that bit deep into my libido.

'Rico can't touch me,' she said.

'Especially if you're in New York,' I said.

She broke down a bit then. Something was happening inside her that I couldn't reach, some internal struggle that she alone could put to rights. 'It isn't easy to make a break, Mike. I've got nobody to go to for advice.'

'You've got me.'

'But I hardly know you.'

'Try me.'

'You make it sound awfully easy,' she said.

'And you're working too hard to make it tough. A gal like you can knock them dead in a town the size of New York. Chicago is a backyard compared to what goes on back home. You'll be in the capital of show business, Toni, the hot spot of the world for all performers. I've seen girls with half of what you got making the bigtime there. You can't miss.'

I could feel her come alive under my talk, melting into me and softening as she let me know she was close to me. I was throwing her everything in my book. She was something I wanted, right away, tonight, and on the train to New York.

'You sound as though you really mean it,' Toni said softly.

I showed her that I meant it. I leaned over and kissed her. She sank against me, bringing her right arm up to my neck and letting me feel her fingertips. She gave me her lips and they were mantraps, ripe and yielding.

We were low on the cushion, but I could see over the edge of the wheel, enough to bring the festooned doorman into focus. He was staring our way and scratching his head. He scowled and gawked and took a tentative few steps our way, his beefy frame moving in the stride of the professional pug, a rolling gait that made him seem more apelike than ever. He walked down the pavement and reached the bluestone drive, but some-thing held him there. He came to a sudden halt and his face was so close that I could see the struggle for decision going on in his elemental brain.

'Elmo won't come,' Toni said with conviction.

And she was right. He was standing stiff and dumb. He had his hat off and was working away at his head, scratching for an extra moment. Then he turned abruptly and strode back to his former position at the door, as idiotic as a caged chimpanzee in the zoo. I leaned over her. 'What do you say, Toni?'

'You're a hard man to brush off.'

'You'll be there?'

'I'm sold, Mike.'

She stepped out of the car and started up the driveway and she didn't look back to wave good-bye. I caught a last squint of her as I turned my car around. The big doorman stepped aside to let her enter the house. She didn't say a word to him.

4

Union Station, Chicago
5:03 P.M. — July 17th

I put Toni aboard the train and saw that
she was comfortable, and went out again
to the appointed meeting place with John
Gilligan. He appeared at the exact
moment of our appointment, as punctual
as an anxious lover. He was dressed
meticulously, the picture of an English
country gentleman in casual tweeds and a
fuzzed Tyrolian sport hat. He looked as
young as I, the lucky stiff, despite the fact
that he was on the edge of the fattening
forties. But Gilligan was the type of
aristocratic gent who would never thicken
around the gizzard or add too many
furrows and wrinkles to his smooth and
sharp-etched face. Crossing the station on
the way to me, he bounced with a spry
and confident step, smooth and athletic.
He held the same collegiate pipe clamped

firmly in his lips. He greeted me with a steel grip and a professional smile, complete with a full display of his dentures.

'No luggage, Wells?' he asked.

'I always travel light,' I said. 'I've got plenty of stuff in New York.'

'This trip will be a lark for you. Sometimes I envy you private investigators. Years ago, when I was in college, I had active dreams of becoming a member of your brotherhood. What easier way to earn money than simply pursuing a fat man?'

'The law,' I said. 'For my dough, you legal beagles have the racket.'

'You're not serious?' He was profoundly shocked at my deadpan comeback. 'The law is an intricate business, Wells.'

'Not when you have retainers like Rico Bruck. I'll bet he's paying you a big bundle of cabbage every year just for holding his hand, as the feller says.'

Gilligan didn't respond to my ribbing. He had his eyes aimed at the gate. His expression reminded me of the beady squint of a thoughtful animal, but not a beast of the active kind. He was a sloth, a skinny sloth, on the lookout for a vagrant morsel of game. We were in the shadows. We were hidden from the view of all passing pedestrians bound for the Century. But Gilligan cased the crowd with an alert eye, and nobody he wanted to observe could ever escape his fixed focus.

He nudged my arm. There was a ponderous figure moving across the open area before us.

'The fat man,' said Gilligan.

'Fat?' I asked. 'He's a moving mountain.'

'An accurate description, Wells.'

'He'll be easy,' I said. 'You were right about him, Gilligan. It'll be like following an elephant through the lobby of the Ritz.'

The fat man wasn't really fat. He was big and broad and beefy and stout. He was a giant. He had great square shoulders and a head to match, straight-lined above the collar so that he gave you the feeling he had no neck at all. There are degrees of avoirdupois. The flabby fat man waddles, overburdened with too much weight in the wrong places, around the navel and in the stomach so that basic movement becomes a serious problem and the simple chore of walking resembles a hippopotamus on the prowl through the jungle. My man was different. I couldn't see his face, but he moved with surprising agility for a man of his girth. He wore a massive trench coat of the lighter-shaded variety, a creation that gave him the appearance of a military mogul. At the gate he paused for a quick turn to look behind him, but his features were lost to me because of the intervening crowds. Then he was gone down the ramp.

'Think you can miss him?' Gilligan asked with a wry smile.

'That would be impossible. There isn't another one like him alive.'

'You're quite right. You noticed, of course, that he, too, carries no luggage. Does that mean anything to you?'

'It could mean that he's got a nest in New York somewhere.'

'Exactly my theory.' He grinned and looked at his watch. 'I must be off now, Wells. Good luck to you. I'll see you in New York.'

I watched him stride away, an aristocratic figure, as jaunty and self-contained as a State Department official on a welcoming committee. Then I wandered to the news-stand, bought a paper and studied the inside pages for more news of the Folsom case. The mess had simmered down. There was a small notice on the fourth page, an item from the D.A.'s, office, a few planted words explaining that the Chicago beagles were still at work on the deal and were making progress. The words brought a chuckle to my throat.

I skipped down the ramp and into the train.

Toni was waiting for me, dressed in a provocative ensemble designed to feature the elegance of her figure.

'Where were you?' she pouted.

'I had to see a man about a man,' I said.

'For a minute I thought the train would be leaving without you.'

'Do I look *that* crazy?'

'Not crazy,' Toni said, 'but maybe busy in the head. You look that way right this minute. What's bothering you?'

'You.'

'Character,' she said and let me kiss her. She had already ordered a pair of drinks, remembering my taste for Scotch. 'Sit down and relax and tell me all about it.'

The train rolled out of the station and we had two more of the same before we got up and went into the diner for dinner. We were planted at an end table, so that I could case the place as we ate, alert and anxious for another squint at the fat man. But he didn't show. We completed our meal and sat there nursing more liquid nourishment and running through a breakdown of Toni's dreams for success in New York. I was operating out of my yen for a close-up of Fat Boy, holding her there in the hope that I might get to know his face.

A table on a train promotes intimacy. The wheels sang beneath us and the black square of the window was a frame for the skittering rush of lights outside. We drank black coffee and made passes at each other with our eyes.

'Another drink?' I asked.

'I fall asleep when I drink too much, Mike.'

'Have some more coffee.'

'Maybe I won't need any more if we leave now.'

We strolled back through a section of coaches, and I found myself working my eyes over the passengers again. I saw nothing of the fat man. Curiosity gnawed at me. Once, on another assignment, I had followed a little man named Pradow, a wealthy merchant who had suddenly decided to escape from the stifling company of his wife and four small children. Pradow had boarded a train, too, but the sneaky crumb had pulled a switch with me. He had walked into the train, all right. But he had also walked out, a simple strategy that slowed up my chase for a full week before I could pick up his scent again.

A seasoned eye takes no chances. I paused at the door to our drawing room, making up my mind about the fat man. He had entered the train a full ten minutes before I walked in behind him.

48

He could have slipped out during that time. He might be laughing at me right now, in some convenient bar in Chicago. A seasoned eye doesn't welcome that type of laughter.

Toni came to the door and put a hand on me.

'Still thinking?' she asked.

'I'll turn it off in a few minutes,' I promised.

'Now,' said Toni, and pulled me around so that I could look at her through the door. 'Or never.'

She was standing there and playing games with her eyes. And yawning. I made my decision. I followed her inside.

'Getting sleepy?' I asked.

'It's only ten o'clock. I just didn't want you standing out there.'

'Trains always knock me out. I think too much on trains.'

'Why all the thought?'

'Maybe it's the sound of the wheels,' I explained, watching her at work with her hand mirror, powdering her nose. 'They have a soporific effect on me.'

'Watch your language,' Toni commented.

'What's with the powder?'

'My nose is too shiny.'

'Too shiny for what?' I took the mirror from her. 'Save it for later, Toni.'

'Later?'

'Tomorrow morning.'

'You're rushing me again,' she pouted.

'You said you liked it slow and easy, remember?'

'What a salesman you are.'

'Are you buying?' I had her hand and she didn't resist me. Her palm was slightly damp.

'Coax me.'

'Sit down,' I said, and tugged her my way. She rolled into my arms and let me kiss her. The compact dropped on the carpet with a flat slap.

'Slow and easy,' Toni said. 'And let's get comfortable, please.'

Far up ahead the whistle of the train screamed twice. The silence grew around us and I reached backward, groping along the wall until I found the light switch and clicked it off. Her yielding body told me that this was what she wanted.

Suddenly I felt Toni tighten in my

arms. Her body strained against mine and her hands came down to my chest and she was clawing me, pushing me back and staring past me toward the door. In the semi-gloom, her eyes were wide with alarm as she watched the door. Whatever she was looking at had scared her into a frozen, heart-pounding horror. She was whispering something to me. I turned around to follow her eyes.

And then I saw the silhouette in the door.

It was the fat man.

'Good evening,' he said.

5

Twentieth Century Limited
10:06 P.M. — July 17th

I switched on the light.

Up close he was bigger than big in the electric moment of his entrance, I found myself torn between shock and laughter. Not that I would have laughed at him. He didn't encourage hilarity. His heavy brows were lowered in a queasy scowl and his eyes were deep slits beneath them, in which a bright spark burned with a steady, intense flame. The expression on his face was rigged to raise the hackles of any ardent lover caught, as I was, between the immediate present and the delectable future with Toni.

I said, 'You're in the wrong room, Chubby.'

'Am I?'

He was staring hard at Toni, enjoying her frantic effort to button her blouse. He uttered an indecent laugh.

'You fat slob!' Toni said.

'Temper,' said the fat man. He had a soft voice for a man of his bulk, an oily voice, a voice that bit because it did not bark, loaded with the undertones of habitual authority, the quality of offi-ciousness, the sharpness of accustomed poise. 'The little lady has a bad temper.'

'So has this little man,' I said.

'Kick the fat bum out, Mike.'

'My apologies,' said the fat man. He looked again at Toni and his mean lips curled disdainfully at the edges, adding no humor to the sly and evil sparkle of his eyes. 'My deepest apologies, young lady. But I'm staying.'

'Why here?' I asked angrily.

'Why not?'

'Because we don't want a third for pinochle, Chubby.'

Was he off his rocker? Sometimes a man with a fixed idea can be loosened and lightened by a touch of comedy. But this character did not respond to my gag file. He chuckled briefly, a small surge of amusement that collapsed before it got

53

underway, a stock laugh that could indicate thin contempt as well as merriment. He continued to stare at Toni until she was forced to squirm in her seat and avoid his eyes, overcome by their probing contempt.

'I do not play pinochle,' he said.

'I'll scout around in the lounge and get you a poker game,' I said.

He shook his head at me, unsmiling. 'No cards, my friend.'

'A kick, Mike,' said Toni. 'What he wants is a good kick in his fat — '

'Temper,' said the fat man again.

There was an element of unreality in his pose. He stood there appraising us and what came through his eyes resembled the calculated coolness of a madman. Was he really nuts? What psychiatric upheaval gnawed at his brain? His brittle smile was doing things to my blood pressure. I began to sweat. Anger and impatience tightened me.

'You heard the lady,' I shouted. 'So you made a mistake and wandered into the wrong room. Now beat it.'

He didn't beat it. He stood there,

grinning down at me, and from where I sat his tremendous body gained power and stature out of the forced perspective.

'Suppose I tell you that I am not in the wrong room?' he asked quietly.

'You want to see my tickets?'

'Not at all.'

'You want me to call the porter?'

'I only want you to stay where you are.'

He had a face to frighten babies, built king-size, with fleshy jowls and ruddy cheeks. His great trench coat was big enough to clothe a dozen midgets. His fat neck almost buried the neat and conservative tie, a simple design in blue, selected to set off the gray suiting that showed a bit higher up near the lapels. His face was cut in classic lines, with a short, sharp nose and a small, cruel mouth. But it was his eyes that held you. They were black and burning and buried behind the deep shadows of his brows. They were highlighted by a pinpoint glow of some reflected radiance — the eyes of a huge bird, a rapacious vulture. His baleful stare annoyed me.

I got up.

'I would suggest that you remain seated,' he said gently.

'And I suggest you wiggle your fat ass out of here,' I told him. 'Fun is fun, but I'm not in the mood for games.'

'I assure you,' the fat man said, eyeing Toni with something resembling humor, 'that I am not jesting. Not in the least. I intend to remain in this room.'

'*Out!*' I shouted, moving in close to his beefy frame. 'Beat it.'

He didn't move. He stood there, only two feet away from me, but his massive body made the distance seem insignificant. I hesitated for a small tick of time, pondering a way to level the big crud. In the pause I saw Toni press the button for the porter. I aimed a fist at his jaw.

He caught my hand and I found myself squirming in his grasp. He had iron bands in his arm, a viselike grip that challenged my muscles. I swung up at him with my free arm, but he caught it with the skill of a seasoned pug, turned me around and put the pressure on my wrist so that a bolt of pain skittered along the edge of my shoulder, as sharp as a knife stab. He had me in the position used for mayhem, a judo hold that limited my movements so that he could break my arm at any time the mood inspired him. I kicked out at him and felt my shoe connect with his shin. He uttered a growled obscenity and squeezed me hard again. I yelped with pain. Then there was a knock on the door.

The fat man glared at me. He slapped me forward so that I fell alongside Toni. There was a gun in his hand suddenly, a small and evil-looking automatic, aimed at my nose.

'Now be quiet,' he said, 'while I answer the door.'

He backed up and opened the door a wide crack.

'Anything wrong, sir?' the porter asked.

'Nothing at all,' laughed the fat man. 'Just a friendly little argument, son.'

'I thought I heard somebody yelling out, sir.'

'You certainly did,' the big man chuckled. 'Everybody shouts these days when you talk politics. Don't you? I rang for a nightcap, but we've changed our minds about it. My friends and I are going to play a bit of gin rummy. Here's a buck for your trouble.'

The porter mumbled his thanks and the door closed. The fat man stood over us.

He said, 'Kindly move closer to your companion, my friend. I'd prefer to be facing both of you. We must not have another flurry of that sort, for I'm too nervous with a gun in my hand. I'd recommend that you sit quite still and do not excite me.'

Toni squeezed her trembling knee against mine to tell me that she was afraid.

'What's the gag?' I asked.

'Gag? There is no gag.'

'What do you want?'

'The pleasure of your company.'

'You mean you're not leaving?'

'Not tonight,' said the fat man. And once again he aimed his eyes at Toni in an appreciative flick. 'Sorry that I must ruin your fun, old fellow.'

6

Twentieth Century Limited
10:35 P.M. — July 17th

The fat man sat down: squatting, the giant trench coat bunched up around his shoulders, giving him the appearance of a great animal, crouched and ready for anything that might move against him. His cold eyes held us in focus with a sharpness and unblinking keenness that brought the shivers to Toni's shanks again. I started one hand down to comfort her.

'Up,' said the fat man. 'I want your hands where I can see them, son.'

'Anything else you want?'

'Only peace and quiet.' He let himself slide into a more comfortable position while he reached into his jacket pocket and took a small card from his wallet. He held the card in his pudgy fingers and stared at it smilingly, as though it might contain a printed joke that he alone could understand. 'I am a prosaic businessman in an unorthodox situation. I can understand your incredulity, young man, but there is little you can do about it, I assure you. We might just as well remain in good temper.'

He slid the business card along the table top so that I could read it:

SIDNEY WRAGGE
Importing — Exporting
Kimberly Building — New York

I fingered the card, but I was staring beyond it at the strong highlight on the muzzle of his automatic.

'To be specific,' he continued, 'let me say that I am pursuing a course that will ensure me a temporary haven for the night.'

'Why doesn't he talk English?' Toni said, her fear diminishing as she read the card.

Sidney Wragge only lifted an eyebrow at her comment before continuing. 'I am following the old rule that there is always safety in numbers.'

'Safety from what?' I asked.

'Death,' said Sidney Wragge.

He closed his eyes on the word, smiling at it, savoring it as Toni gasped and started to shiver again. He leaned back, a mountain of placidity. The train clacked on through the night and the boxed stillness of our little cubicle built the tension in me. I had to study the gorilla, fascinated by his closeness. He was wearing an ancient diamond stickpin in his tie, an archaic ornament, one bright stone surrounded by a circle of small emeralds. Was this a clue to his age? I figured him to be in his forties. He could be an Englishman or a Canadian from the way he spouted his dialogue. But where did he get his power? I had wrestled the beefy boys, lots of them, when I was in the army. I had handled his type before. Yet Sidney Wragge had something all the others lacked against me. He used his bulk only as a foundation for his huge and dynamic hands. The tremendous paw that held the gun was neat and clean and well-manicured. He was grinning at me, his eyes wise, his thin lips curled in a mocking smile.

I said, 'Somebody wants to bump you off?'

'Precisely.'

'And you're sure he's on this train?'

'Quite sure.' His free hand went down into the pocket of his trench coat and when he lifted it, there was a candy in it. He popped the candy into his mouth, moving his jaw slowly and pursing his lips as he sucked at its flavor. 'Life Savers,' he said. 'Care to join me?'

'Nuts,' I said. 'And nuts to your story, Wragge.'

'You don't believe me?'

'You sound like something out of a bad movie.'

Sidney Wragge shrugged casually. 'Death is often unbelievable, my boy. There are significant shadings of value in the semantics of death. Being killed is a day-to-day risk that all of us take in our civilized meanderings. A man may be killed while crossing the street, riding an elevator, or shaving his chin.' He paused to allow me to follow the direction of his philosophic double talk. 'A man who is running from death must take chances. That is why I am sitting here at this moment.'

'What did he say?' Toni asked.

'He says he's afraid of being killed,' I explained.

'Why doesn't he tell the conductor and shake his fat tail out of here?'

'Hah,' said Sidney Wragge. 'The young lady has a sense of humor.'

'Drop dead,' Toni commented. 'If I was afraid of being killed, I'd be smart enough to figure that this is a big train, a hell of a big train, fat boy, with a lot of people on it. Maybe even a couple of cops. All you have to do is walk outside and pull the emergency cord and the train will stop. Take a flying jump into the nearest swamp — and leave us alone.'

Sidney Wragge lost himself in an outburst of husky laughter, a real yak, enough to make his fleshy jowls quiver. He wound it all up in a fit of coughing, out of control, the high blood pressure alive on his cheeks.

'A truly original sense of humor,' he gasped. 'The young lady is really talented.

Perhaps that is why I prefer to remain where I am.' He examined a gold wrist watch. 'It is getting quite late, my friends. I'd suggest that you both try for some sleep.'

'Do I look double-jointed?' Toni asked.

'You will gain nothing by remaining awake,' said Wragge.

'You don't inspire slumber,' I said. 'Nor does that fowling piece you're aiming at us.'

'You must put it out of your mind, my friend. Forget about my presence here.'

'You're too fat to forget,' Toni said.

Sidney Wragge shrugged and popped another Life Saver into his mouth. Now, as he turned his head to stare out of the window, I found myself itching with the sudden urge to sketch him, to put him down on paper for my collection of criminal studies.

Sidney Wragge's head, in profile, brought his personality into truer perspective. Front face, he could be a kindly man — Mr. Babbitt, the head of a successful corporation. But in profile the cut of his features brought out the hardness in him. His eyes, deep hidden under the shaggy brows, gave his head the keen and predatory look of an evil bird, an eagle, a falcon, a hawk. His grayed brows were unkempt and uncombed in a John L. Lewis effect, falling in disorder over the dark pits that screened his eyes.

I reached into my pocket for my tiny sketch book, but the gun was up off the table and aimed at my head before the gesture was completed.

'Down,' said Sidney Wragge. 'Keep your hands on the table.'

'If I had a gun, I would have used it a long time ago,' I said.

'You want a cigarette?' he asked, offering me a deck of Parliaments. 'Have one of mine.'

'Go to hell,' I told him.

He lit a cigarette and said nothing. Outside, the landscape fled by our window, a black panel punctuated by little dots of light. Already Toni had slumped over the table, her head in her arms, her blonde hair poured over the tabletop. Soon she was asleep and breathing in a restful pattern. But my innate stubbornness would not allow me to join her. I half-closed my eyes and gave myself up to a game of cat and mouse.

If I could catch him off guard, I might disarm him in a rush. I watched him patiently, a fogged figure through the narrowing slit of my left eye. I estimated the level at which I would hit him. If I aimed low, I could get him in the gut, knocking the breath out of him and grab the gun. He held it on his knee now, and I thought I saw it waver slightly, as though he himself might be dozing off . . .

I pretended to sleep deeply. I began to snore to prove it, wheezing and blubbering my imitation so that it might convince him. The muscles in my legs were tight knots as I prepared to use them, counting off the minutes as they crawled by. When I thought twenty minutes had passed, I steeled myself for the lunge at him. Now.

And then Sidney Wragge laughed.

'Amateurish,' he chuckled, bringing the gun up so that the muzzle rested on my cheek. 'A very amateurish performance, my friend. The next time you wish to feign sleep, you must not snore so soon or so loud. You should learn, too, how to control your reflexes. When I coughed a moment ago your fingers moved slightly, an unnatural reaction for a man who snores so sincerely. I assume that you've been planning to disarm me? I suggest you abandon that strategy. I have an uncanny ability to remain awake indefinitely.'

I gave up the game two hours later.

And after that, sleep slapped me down.

7

Twentieth Century Limited — New York
8:14 A.M. — July 18th

I awoke when the train was rolling down
through the tenement section of Park
Avenue. I awoke but I didn't move. On
my right, Toni still sprawled in sleep. The
sound of the wheels softened into a dull
rumbling beat as the tunnel closed in on
us, and above the noise of the train's
movement I struggled for some small
signal that would tell me that Sidney
Wragge was still with us. The signal came.
Under the table, his foot moved, slowly,
carefully, quietly, but close enough so that
the edge of his shoe touched mine as he
slipped smoothly out of his seat.

I allowed him the time to start for the
door.

Then I leaped.

I hit him low in a flying tackle, and he
grunted his surprise as he fell forward

against the door, a mountain of flesh. He was caught off guard, but the springs in his legs came to life suddenly, kicking out at me so that my hands slid away from his beefy thighs. He had his back turned to me, yet before he adjusted his massive frame for the continuance of our struggle, I knew that the little automatic was in his right hand. He made the thought a fact. He brought the gun down hard, missing my head, but slapping my shoulder so that it stung with a thousand needles of pain. It forced me back, but I managed to lay one into his midsection, a short right that would have floored any other fat man on earth but Sidney Wragge. My fist hit nothing soft. I had expected the flabby gut found on most obese characters. Instead, his larded midsection was firm and muscled, as though he was a boxer in shape for an important match. He was working me over now, trying for another crack at me with the gun. The crack came. He hit me on the side of the head, above the ear. I heard his husky chuckle as I began to fall, a deep-throated laugh that faded and died by the time I hit the floor.

After that, Toni was slapping me awake.

The darkness cleared and the room swam back into focus. I looked first through the window, watching the concrete wall slide slowly away as the train rolled into Grand Central Station.

'He almost murdered you!' Toni was saying.

'But not quite,' I said, struggling to my feet. The muscles in my legs had turned to butter. I slapped out at my shanks and worked myself into a standing position. 'I'm lucky, Toni. The train must have been tied up in the tunnel. I'm going after that stinker.'

'Why bother?' Toni argued. 'You'll fall flat on your fanny if you chase him. You're knocked out, Mike.'

I grabbed my hat. 'I'll meet you at the Brentworth Hotel,' I said. 'See you later.'

I ran out into the corridor. The train had stopped a minute ago and a crowd of passengers clogged the exits. I pushed and shoved my way to the door, disregarding the unkind words thrown my way. Out on the ramp, the mob swelled in the catacombs leading up the station. I threaded a broken course through them and ran into the broad arena of the station.

I saw him then.

He was moving fast, his huge figure tilted stiffly forward in the stride of a retreating admiral, bound for the Vanderbilt Avenue exit. I raced after him, giving him his head but cutting down his lead so that I was boarding the cab behind him when he pulled away. He headed uptown to the middle Sixties on the East Side, and got out at one of the old apartment houses that lined the street. I left my cab a few hundred feet behind him and crossed the street to note the number of his place. Then I backtracked quickly to the corner and ducked into the drugstore.

A thin and pimply youth dispensed a soft drink for me. It was a tiny trap, a combination drug and luncheonette of the type that supplies a neighborhood with everything from antihistamine to lawn seed.

'The boss in?' I asked.

'I'm him,' said the youth.

'You own this store?'

He looked up from the sink slop and gave me the dregs of his disregard, as sad-eyed as a sick cow. 'What are you, a tax collector, mister? I tell you, this is my place. Period.'

'For how long?'

'How long, he's asking me,' he said to the rag in his hands. 'All this for a nickel coke? All right. I've been here two years. You happy?'

'I'm tickled to death,' I told him. 'Because you can help me with some information. I'm looking for a friend of mine and I can't seem to find him. A fat man. You know him, maybe?'

He wiped his hands and thumbed his chin and stared at the ceiling. Druggists are the most helpful merchants on earth to the private eye brigade. They had helped me before on many occasions, especially when the hunt involved a hideout or a stray. The local pill and powder emporiums cater to a broad mass of customers, who come in regularly for their accustomed medicaments and occasional cigarettes and soft drinks. A druggist with a brain and a memory can cut down a chase and simplify the threads that lead to the quarry. From where I sat the entrance to the apartment where the fat man had disappeared was in focus for me. I kept my eye on that door and watched. Nobody stirred down there.

'A fat man from around here?' the druggist asked himself. And then it came to him. He snapped his fingers and something resembling the spark of life entered his watery eyes. 'Of course. Down the block?'

'He lives around here, then?'

'Number 465. Over there.' He pointed to the house I watched.

'You remember his name?'

'Sidney.'

'Then you know him well?'

'I know Sidney, all right.' He studied the glass he was polishing for a moment. He was making up his mind about something, a problem that forced him into the original pose, the bovine speculation that suited him so well. 'He a friend of yours?'

'Sidney and I are pals.'

He leaned over the counter. He took off his glasses and began to heat them with his breath and polish them. He returned them to the bridge of his long nose and stared at me. 'Do you want him for a bet, mister? He makes book for you, too?'

'Sid and I are in the same line,' I said, grabbing the hook and holding it. Sometimes a private eye spends four weeks working up to a lead like this. Other times the gods are kind, and the check-up is easy. 'I just got into town from Chicago and figured I'd stop in and chew the fat with Sid. You been betting with him long?'

'Couple of months,' the druggist said. 'But he hasn't showed up lately.'

'Listen, do you know where I can get him? You know his hangouts?'

'I know nothing about him.'

'His friends, maybe?'

He hesitated, chewing his lip while throwing me occasional sly and jerky glances. He was making up his mind about something. But it would take a full day for him to come to any conclusion at the rate his feeble intellect meshed its gears. He lit a cigarette nervously and mixed himself a cherry drink. He sipped it, studying the bubbles.

'You remember one of his friends?' I asked.

'No. But I was just thinking. You want to take a bet for me?'

'I don't want Sid's customers,' I said. 'I don't operate that way.'

But he was reaching into his pants and producing two dog-eared dollar bills. 'What do you care?' he asked laughingly. 'Sid isn't here to take my money. So why shouldn't you? Put this on Lady Lombar in the fifth at Belmont.'

'A dog,' I said. 'Lay off the nag. Take my advice.'

He reddened around the ears as though I had insulted his mother. 'Never mind the advice, mister. I bet what I bet. Lady Lombar in the fifth. You taking it?'

So I took it. He came alive after I had pocketed his dough, a typical reaction of the horse player who has done his duty to his conscience. Sometimes you do a man a favor by taking his loot. The small-time gambler burns with the yen to get one bet down each day, his ritual battle with the gods of chance. And from the way this goon acted, Lady Lombar would go off a long shot and he was already rejoicing at her victory. He poured me another drink, this one on the house. He expanded for me.

'That Sid,' he said. 'He's got the business. Does he book much?'

'Plenty,' I lied. 'Sid's loaded.'

'You'd never know it, would you? I mean, the way he acts — just a nice fat guy minding his own business. Only time I figured him for the bigtime dough was when he came in here with that broad of his.'

'A broad?' I asked, putting on a show of surprise. 'Sid's been holding out on me. Built?'

'But stacked. What I'd give for a dame like that.'

'Good old Sid,' I commented. 'He never told me.'

'I don't blame him a bit. Listen, if I had a babe like that one, I'd build a wall around her. She's just about the hottest-looking doll you ever laid your eyes on — '

'Listen, you wouldn't know her name? I

could pull a big gag on old Sid if I knew who she was.'

'Her name?' he asked himself. 'Let me think a minute, mister.'

He thought it over. He closed his eyes and bit his lip again and ran his dirty fingernails through his dirty hair. He stared at a bird on a hydrant across the street. He sucked and puffed at his cigarette. He scratched his head and made faces at the floor, and when it was all over he lit up with a small but significant spark of animation.

'Spain,' he said. 'Linda Spain, a burlesque broad. You ever heard of her? She's terrific, mister. Go down to the old Braddock Theatre some night, behind the alley, because the place is closed up in front. For three bucks they'll let you in to watch the girls shake it. Listen, this babe is the hottest — '

'Thanks,' I said. 'I'll see you tomorrow, if Lady Lombar breezes in.'

8

The Brentworth was an ancient trap, a relic of the early days of the century, located in the middle Forties. Its rococo facade had been sandblasted recently, so that the front stood out among the dismal rows of office buildings flanking it. The lobby blossomed with the latest in modern decor, a decorator's dream of delight, complete with striated woods and startling niches. But the customers looked as old as the foundation of the building. A few wrinkled faces paused in the perusal of their morning newspapers to look up and examine me as I breezed to the desk. It struck me that I had seen brighter faces at the morgue.

The desk man informed me that the 'young lady' was waiting for me upstairs in my suite, 904, and he hoped that my stay in New York would be pleasant. He was a dapper, efficient character, probably the manager. He gave me the best wishes of John Gilligan and hoped my suite was comfortable, and if anything bothered me would I kindly pick up the phone and tell him so that he could make it right for me?

I took the elevator and found number 904. It was a two-room deal, quietly done in pastel shades, with windows facing Broadway so that the Paramount Tower became the center of interest in the ridge of buildings outside.

Toni was waiting for me in a bright yellow lounging outfit that made her look like something out of a fashion ad. She had taken a shower and freshened her make-up, a softer shade now, for daytime wear.

I said, 'Hungry, Toni?'

She led me into the living room and pointed to a tray full of dishes. 'I was starved, Mike. You don't mind?'

'Not a bit. I like my women well fed.'

'How about you?'

'I can do anything better on an empty stomach.'

'I believe you,' Toni said. 'What about the fat man? Did you track him down?'

'I know where I can put my finger on him.'

'A finger wouldn't bother him. He certainly was the fattest man I ever saw in my life. What was with him? You think he was crazy? He sure acted crazy.'

'Like a fox,' I said. 'He's no fool, Toni.'

I picked up the phone, called the Waldorf, and asked for Rico Bruck. Toni was standing at the window when I mouthed his name. She swiveled around and came at me, her face working to show me her sudden surprise. She stood there, watching me in fascination, tonguing her upper lip and breathing hard. Rico was out. I left a message for him and hung up.

'Why didn't you tell me Rico was coming to New York?' Toni asked. She clutched my arm and squeezed it. She was trembling. She was shaking like a Mixmaster, so violently that I grabbed her and patted her where it would do the most good.

'Why didn't you ask me?'

'I don't want him to know I'm here, Mike.'

'He won't know. It'll be our little secret.'

'I ran away from Rico's place to stay clear of things like *this*,' she said. 'I don't want any part of it.'

'You're on the outside,' I told her. 'All I did for Rico was follow that fat character. You told Rico you were quitting?'

'I just walked out, Mike. He's going to be sore as hell if he finds out I'm with you.'

'He'll never know.'

'You're so damned sure of yourself,' Toni said with a weak sob, and walked away from me and into the bedroom. I followed her inside and found her sitting on the bed, her pretty head buried in her hands. 'But you don't know Rico.'

'Tell me about him.'

'He's bad, Mike. He could make it tough for me in New York.'

'Why should he?'

'Just because he's mean, because he expects everybody who works for him to be loyal.' She shivered and showed me her troubled eyes. And when I put my arm around her, there was no warmth to her body. 'He could circulate lousy stories about me here,' Toni said. 'He has all kinds of contacts in show business.'

'You're dramatizing him,' I said. I turned her face my way and looked into her damp eyes. 'Unless you and he were playing rabbit together. Was that it?'

'What do I look like?' she asked angrily, shrugging my hand away. 'I wouldn't be found dead in a bed with him.'

'And he knows it?'

'I've told him often, Mike.'

'I can't blame him for not giving up,' I said, with another try at her waist. This time she allowed me to keep my hand where I put it, around her waist with a gentle pressure. 'But you're all wrong about Rico, Toni — because he'll never know from me that you're in town. Does that help? Or shall I sing it to you?'

'It helps,' Toni said quietly. 'You're a good egg, Mike. I can't help feeling that I can trust you.'

'Is that all you feel?' I pulled her to me and she did not fight.

'Maybe what I feel scares me a little.'

'We're talking too much, Toni,' I said.

She answered with her lips, giving herself to me with a rush of enthusiasm that set the hidden fires burning in me. 'I'm all through talking now,' she said. 'Don't let me talk any more, Mike.'

9

Marty's Bar and Grill — New York
4:23 P.M. — July 18th

I took her to Marty's later. Marty's place was a hangout for the newspaper boys, writers and theatrical folk of the neighborhood, an intimate steak-and-chowderhouse that featured sawdust floors and food that was geared to make you drool. My New York office was around the corner. We sat at the bar and waited for my partner, Izzy Rosen. It was almost five, and Izzy would be in soon.

When the hour arrived Izzy came with it, pushing through the door with his usual burst of energy. He spotted me at the bar and slapped me affectionately while I introduced him to Toni Kaye.

'Glad to meet you,' Toni said, eyeing him with the sly and frigid regard of a judge at a dog show. 'Any friend of Mike's is a friend of mine.'

'That goes double,' Izzy beamed. He had a quick and intelligent face, and added her up with no effort at all. And when he had finished his mental gymnastics, he ordered a drink and disregarded her. 'Break down the deal for me, Mike,' he said. 'Maybe you'll be needing me?'

I cut it up into small pieces for him, including the dramatic session on the train and the hurly-burly that had followed. Izzy listened with his accustomed concentration. Up close, he looked for all the world like a prosperous theatrical man: an agent, a producer, or a Broadway entrepreneur. He dressed in the height of style, featuring the latest in masculine apparel: clothes that built his dumpy frame into a picture of middle-class prosperity. He could have been somebody's tailor; a well-to-do cloak-and-suiter. He could have been the poor man's Billy Rose, doing the town with a pocketful of loot. But Izzy Rosen was none of these things.

We joined forces five years ago, when I opened the Chicago office. Izzy had proved himself the best private investigator in New

York, a specialist in the finger department, a masterful brain at skip-tracing, tracking down the quarry when it runs for the dim and distant corners. Izzy could make a locate with a minimum of information. He had been the inspiration in the chase for Garrison Carruthers three years ago, when the millionaire playboy chose to run for cover from his nagging wife. Izzy had tracked him down in less than three months, breaking the case wide open on a few leads that wouldn't have inspired anyone but himself.

'Fifteen hundred clams for that kind of a chase?' Izzy chuckled and shook his head. 'It doesn't make sense, Mike.'

'Do we ask questions when the bundle is so big?' I asked.

'We do not. You phoned in Sidney Wragge's address to Rico?'

'Rico isn't in his room at the Waldorf.'

'You want me to phone it in?' Izzy asked, rolling his eyes toward Toni in a suggestive grin. 'You're going to be busy this afternoon, I gather?'

'All tied up.' I said. 'Toni and I are going to have some food now, Izzy. You want to keep trying Rico?'

'Whatever you say.'

'Let me know when you reach him. I'll be at the Brentworth late this afternoon.'

'Of course you will,' Izzy smiled.

And he tipped his hat with a fine show of gallantry, downed his drink and marched out of there.

Toni and I sipped black coffee and had a few brandies and smoked a few cigarettes. The place was empty now, save for a few late-afternoon strays who drank at the street end of Marty's bar. We were alone in the back of the bistro, isolated in a small and cozy booth, so that it was possible to mug it up a bit. She leaned against the wall and pulled me to her along the cushioned seat. Her sultry eyes were bright with purpose now. It was no hardship to kiss her.

I said, 'We're wasting time here, Toni.'

'That's what I was thinking, Mike.'

'Pull yourself together, we're going back to the Brentworth.'

We walked the few blocks back to the hotel, and her arm was tight in mine. Even the old cruds in the lobby gazed at her with obvious ardor, following us as we crossed to the elevator and started upstairs. She stopped in the hallway near our door and turned to me.

'Easy, Toni,' I said. 'We're almost home.'

And then I opened the door and the mood left me.

And passion died for Toni at the same moment.

Because we stepped across the threshold into a scene of horror. Everything in the place was upended and loused into disorder: chairs on their sides, tables upset, and the two lamps cracked and smashed on the rug, one of them incongruously lit and glowing with a brilliance that made the tableau a mad thing, something out of a stage set in a melodrama of blood and vengeance. Near the table, his gory head partly covered by the decorative throw, lay the body of a man. He was brutally mangled, his face smashed as though a hundred horses had stomped on it.

'The fat man,' Toni gasped, clutching me. 'The fat man.'

She fainted after that.

10

Toni was out, as cold as a box. I slapped her wrists and tried the water cure until her eyelids quivered and she came alive, shivering her unrest, still caught up by the shock and shudder of her last wakeful moment at the door. The room was bathed in gloom.

'Is he dead?' she whispered.

'I haven't checked,' I said. 'Sit still and grab hold of yourself while I look.'

Sidney Wragge lay on his back, his arms outstretched in a last violent gesture, as though his larded hands had been groping for his assailant's throat. I bent over him, knowing that he was dead before I felt for his pulse. No man could have survived the terrible mauling that had floored Sidney Wragge. The sight of the mess that was once his face pushed

89

me away from him, tortured by gut jumps that almost sent me out of control. I pulled the table cover over his gory head and stood there gawking down at him. The emeralds in his ancient stickpin glimmered at me like malevolent eyes. On my knees, I lifted his trench coat gently. It was not buttoned. Wragge must have visited at his ease, loosening his coat as he strolled my room. I reached inside his jacket and found his wallet — empty. Somebody had cleaned him thoroughly.

'What are we going to do?' Toni asked from the door, sobbing now, blubbering like a schoolgirl caught in a fraternity house. 'This'll be the end of me, Mike. You've got to take me out of here. Nobody will want me in show business if this gets out. Please — '

I went to her and shook her gently, cutting her prelude to hysteria before it ripened into the real thing.

I said, 'This thing stinks to high heaven, Toni. We're in it up to our ears.'

'Why can't we run?'

'Run? How far? You remember the porter on the train last night? He's going to remember us, baby. He's also going to recall the fact that we had a visitor in the drawing room. The city dicks will add this one up as fast as a belch after a beer.'

She was sobbing quietly, her head buried in her hands, not listening to me at all. My mind sloughed her off, busy with the mechanics of the moment, the inevitable headache that was blooming inside of me, goosed along by the rush of anger that beat at me whenever I added it all up. My jittery brain worked over the events of last night, backtracking through the drama in the drawing room, reliving the scene with Sidney Wragge, bleeding it for clues to his strange behavior. What lunatic urge had brought Wragge to my rooms? My mind brought him back into focus: all of him, including his forthright dialogue, his prickling fear of death, his powerful stubbornness.

I ran back to the bedroom. Toni's bag lay opened in the corner of the room, beyond the bed, its contents strewn over the rug as though a strong wind had blown her undergarments there. The lock was cracked, prodded into a twisted mess by a powerful hand probably wielding a penknife. She went over her intimate belongings with me. There was nothing missing.

'Wragge probably hid the pendant in your bag last night,' I said. 'It would have been easy for him while we were asleep. He came back here to pick up the cluster while we were out. But somebody knew he was coming. He must have been tailed from his flat.'

I was talking to myself again, trying for some order out of the debris. I picked up the phone and called Izzy. He was out. Then I called the Waldorf again. Rico was still away. Outside, the city was slipping into darkness, and the Paramount Building was no longer a slender silhouette against the sky. The big clock told me that it was after eight. I had been standing around for a long time. Too long.

'Clean the mascara off your face, Toni,' I said. 'We're getting out of here.'

'Where?' she asked. 'Where are we headed?'

'Out. I've got to make contact with Izzy Rosen. It'll be some time before they find the fat slob up here. And before they do, we've got some calls to make.'

She jumped into action, glad of the chance to leave the bloody room. We slipped into the hall and made the fire stairs without being seen. We went down slowly, pausing on each landing for footsteps. Nobody bothered us. We made the basement and strolled through it, threading our way between the gray pillars and toward the light on the far right. There was a blue bulb glowing at the exit, a door that led into an alley. We entered a canyon of quiet and advanced toward the street. It occurred to me that this would be an easy pitch for a purposeful prowler. Whoever had killed Sidney Wragge might have entered the Brentworth this way, creeping along the alley unobserved and climbing to the ninth floor to do his dirty deed.

My reflections were jolted when we stepped out into the quiet street.

A few yards away a man stood at the curbing, leaning against the sleek chassis of a black sedan. I tugged Toni to one side, planning a detour to the left to avoid him. Standing in the shadows, he was somehow a familiar figure. He turned a toothpick nervously in his hard mouth. He had a lean and a bony jaw to match his angular body. He eased himself away from the car and slipped our way before I could step aside.

'In the car,' he said.

'We're walking, chum,' I said.

'In,' he said again. 'And no tricks.'

I brought my fist up, but he was as agile as a tomcat on the prowl for a mouse. He slapped down at me, and there was a gun in his hand — it caught me on the wrist and paralyzed me, in a vicious swipe that almost brought me to my knees. He kicked out at me, and his foot found my stomach and doubled me up. There was no sound from Toni. He had already grabbed her and pushed her away, into the car, where somebody else held her.

'Now we'll play it all over again,' he said. 'Get up and move. Into the car.'

He had a low voice, guttural and flat. In the darkness I couldn't see much of his face, but once again the feel of him, the timbre of his graveled snarl, stabbed at some recent memory. I had met this gunsel before. He dug the muzzle of his automatic into my navel.

'Next time I'll hurt you,' he said. 'So get in.'

I got in.

11

Lexington Avenue — New York
9:00 P.M. — July 18th

The car roared off, turning sharply into Lexington Avenue and heading uptown. The driver rolled it at a dignified speed. He had stepped into the front seat as soon as he saw me enter the rear of the car. He had the traditional beefy neck of the overweight mobster. I couldn't see the edge of his face. But the man next to Toni and me appeared clearly in the intermittent light from the street. He was close enough for me to smell the weight of his tobaccoed breath, foul and acrid, as he relaxed against the cushions. I caught his profile: lean-nosed and cruel, the face of the professional hard guy, complete with a nasty scar that crawled from his right temple to the sharp line of his upper jaw. Where had I seen him before?

'I know you from somewhere,' I said.

'Peachy,' he said, not bothering to turn my way. 'That's just peachy.'

'Chicago?'

He didn't say. He stared ahead of him, pouting and puffing and playing it dumb. He was coming into focus for me now. I saw him as a newspaper photo, a headlined character in the Folsom mess last week, back in Chicago. I remembered a man of his size and shape pictured alongside Monk Stang, on the way into the courthouse, shielding his head with his hat, a blurred gesture because the camera beat him to the snapshot.

I said, 'Frenchy Armetto. You're making a mistake, Frenchy. You don't want us.'

'Maybe.'

Frenchy Armetto's career carried him into activities in the rod-and-gun department. Frenchy was a smalltime heist man who had been sent down back in 1931 for perpetrating a foolish robbery in Brooklyn. He came out of jail a surly youth, with ambitions to go higher in the world of mayhem and malice. It was at this point in his nefarious life that he joined forces with Monk Stang. Nobody ever did find out whether Frenchy was the lad who shot the two policemen outside the Dugout Club, during the mad larceny of that bistro's coffers one night in 1941. Frenchy was held, but he was never touched. Rumor had it that his alibis were engineered by the great Monk Stang. The press dove into the yarn and tried to spill Monk's guts for the public. But the wily Stang managed to brush away all charges. And, since that day, Monk retired his assistant to the more gentle chores.

And as for Monk himself? No police record held the full display of this man's credits in crime. He was the top man in larceny, certainly, despite the fact that he had abandoned such obvious hijinks more than five years ago. Today Monk Stang devoted himself exclusively to the borderline businesses of crime: the pinball machines, the one-armed bandits, the numbers game, and a few minor dabblings in café-fronted gambling dens, patterned after the models set up by his enemy Rico Bruck. He had no record of mayhem. But what was the reason for the sudden strangling of Archie Fissell, the maggoty czar of all the pinball machines in Brooklyn? Archie was found one night with his tie knotted too tight. It was a small knot, neatly tied, but pulled so snugly around Fissell's neck that the coroner assumed only a giant ape could have applied the pressure. Yet Monk Stang had ripped telephone books in half for the entertainment of his friends. And Monk Stang, by a peculiar coincidence, took over the Fissell territory after that. Without a murmur of protest from the surviving Fissell henchmen.

The same Monk Stang rose to heroic heights during a brawl in his card room behind the Excelsior Garage. On this occasion two newspaper men were witnesses to his ability at grab-and-grunt. In a short but memorable session of fisticuffs, the little flabby-looking mobster had broken the arm of his adversary, and then transported him through the door and into the street, where he was left for the birds.

'Whoever put you on me gave you a bum deal, Frenchy,' I told him, trying for sincerity. 'We just got in from Chicago.

This is our honeymoon.'

He faced me slowly, running his eyes over me in dull appraisal. He followed through to Toni, huddled in the corner, her hand trembling in mine. His mean face broke into a thin-lipped smile, after which he shook his head slightly. He said nothing.

The driver said, 'Save it, mister. You're knocking yourself out.'

'Where are you taking us?'

'Questions,' Frenchy said wearily. 'You ever hear a guy ask so many questions, Max?'

They laughed it up. Frenchy Armetto continued his glum silence after that, chewing his perpetual toothpick as we rolled up Lexington Avenue. The sound of Toni's sobbing filled the car and I gave her a handkerchief and told her to blow her nose and relax. We made a right turn into a residential street in the middle Eighties, quiet and dignified and already half asleep. The car coasted halfway up the block and braked before an ancient residence. Frenchy slid out, and at the same moment the driver had the other

100

door open and was piloting Toni up the stone steps, Frenchy pushed the gun in my ribs and jerked his head toward the entrance. For a quick moment I meditated on making a stab at him. But reason won out over my Boy Scout impulse.

Frenchy prodded us forward and we minced through a narrow hall, gray and dirty and smelling of dampness and the musty backwash of old age and seasoned neglect. Max stood at the stairway, motioning us onward and upward. We climbed the antique stairway, listening to the sound of our footsteps on the rotten boards, Toni's heels setting up a staccato clatter that echoed down the stairwell, while behind us came the shuffling tread of our two captors.

The upstairs hall was narrower and dimmer than the entrance. There was a light perched high on our left, a glassed-in globe, painted a dull red and shimmering with a faded glow. The place stank of decay and corrosion, a zombie residence, like something out of a Charles Addams cartoon, complete with peeling wallpaper and the odor of dry rot.

Our escorts pushed us through the last door on the landing, into a room that seemed incongruous in the house, being as it was neat and clean. Somebody had swept it regularly. And there was a nice desk sitting in the corner, as businesslike as a bank president's. The man who sat behind the desk leaned on his elbow and bit the juice out of a mangled cigar. He squinted up at us curiously, casing Toni quickly and then reserving the full weight of his scrutiny for me.

'Hello, Monk,' I said.

'Do I know you?' he asked.

'You know me.'

'From where?'

'Chicago,' I said. 'You want a hint? You want a crack at the sixty-four-dollar question?'

'A big joke man,' Monk said casually.

What is it that labels the experienced gangster? What special cut of jaw and mouth? What extra fillip of plug-ugly design? Monk Stang violated all the Hollywood rules for criminal casting. He was a middle-aged man of average height and average build. He had an average head, with the average amount of baldness high on the dome, a round spot of scalp, soon to become more barren. Monk had the bearing and gestures of a doctor, a lawyer, a plumber, an accountant. He could have passed as a butcher, a baker, a candlestick maker. You put the pieces together and he added up as a harmless sort of crud, the man in the street, the newsvendor, the haberdasher, the peddler of chestnuts on a busy corner.

You felt the pressure of his personality only when he talked. His voice had a metallic ring, a crisp, brusque finality, an authority that no average man can ever summon up under normal circumstances. And with his voice, the confidence came through in the way he moved. He was moving now, close enough to count the fillings in my upper jaw.

'The courthouse,' I suggested, 'We've met there once or twice, especially on the Lippy Maggee case, two years ago.'

'Sure,' said Monk. 'A private dick?'

'Mike Wells.'

'Sure,' he said again, and stepped back to face Frenchy. 'You positive you got the right guy, Frenchy?'

'He was in the book at the Brentworth,' Frenchy said. 'He was the jerk I saw talking to Gilligan in Chicago, at the station.'

'I don't get it,' Monk said. 'You working for Rico, Wells?'

'I could be,' I said. 'Since when have you been hijacking private investigators, Monk?'

'Frenchy made a mistake,' said Monk, waving away my comment and bending to the task of spitting a pound of loose tobacco shreds from his fat mouth. He advanced to Frenchy and whispered a few subtle comments. Frenchy's voice rose with conviction. The dialogue became heated, so warm that the big chauffeur stepped up behind Monk. Monk pushed him away and yammered at Frenchy.

'Ask the crud,' Frenchy said. 'This private eye was on the train with the fat slob. When he left the train, he tailed the fat boy. Then he came back to the Brentworth. Then he took his girl out to a place called Marty's, over on Lexington. After that, he went back to the Brentworth. Right, Max?'

Max nodded. 'Check, Frenchy. I watched the Brentworth while Frenchy followed this guy to Marty's. I saw the fat man go into the Brentworth. Then, about a half-hour later, this private eye and the broad came back. Me and Frenchy waited for them to come out. They came out.'

'So he must have the stuff,' said Frenchy.

Monk shook his head at me sadly. 'You got the stuff, Wells?'

'What stuff?'

'The gems.'

'I don't know what you're talking about, Monk.'

Monk continued to shake his head with sorrow. 'You want the boys to give you a once-over?'

'You're wasting your time, and mine.'

Frenchy stepped forward and reached for my jacket. It was too much for me. I caught him by the shoulder and slipped him a fast right hook, low enough to take the wind out of his sails. He clutched at his stomach. He said something nasty about my mother, so I hit him again. Toni screamed, but I stepped back and away before Max could reach me. I held my hands over my head and grinned at Max.

'I'm all finished,' I told him. 'That was something I've been wanting to do for the last half-hour. You can frisk me now.'

'Let me at the bastard,' Frenchy said.

Monk reached for him before he could step toward me. 'Save it, Frenchy,' he said. 'You too, Max. This guy is clean. No private dick worth his salt would play gunsel for Rico Bruck. Maybe I owe you an apology, Wells.'

'Stuff it.'

'I don't like my boys playing rough,' Monk said. 'Especially with guys like you, Wells. Listen, stop me if I'm wrong. Rico put you on the fat man's tail. He don't trust his messenger, right? He don't trust the fat boy?'

He was either leveling with me, or he was the best actor in New York City. He was telling me his personal theory about Sidney Wragge — simply, and with a face as straight as a schoolkid reciting the Gettysburg Address. He spouted his last line of dialogue with genuine sincerity, and when I didn't respond, he sat down and waited patiently for my next speech, making a production out of rekindling his dead cigar. He was playing the scene for me alone. He was building it with an instinctive flair for the dramatically apt pauses. But he didn't sell me. How could he? I knew too much of his background.

I said, 'Maybe he didn't. But why would Rico kill the fat boy?'

Monk released a hidden reserve of histrionic ability. He let the cigar fall out of his fingers. He stood up. He leaned on his hands and let his neck jut out my way. He licked his lower lip, twice.

And then he said, 'Did you say the fat boy was knocked off?'

'You heard me, Monk.'

'When? Where?'

So I told him. 'He was murdered in my room at the Brentworth. Maybe an hour or so ago.'

He jumped at the news. He put on a great display of honest surprise, slapping a fist in a palm and pacing the floor and muttering guttural gibberish to promote his befuddlement. He worked hard to show me he was as mystified as I. 'I don't get it,' he said, over and over again. Frenchy Armetto watched his boss with a lynx's eyes, sliding his animal hate my way and accelerating the toothpick in his mouth. The big chauffeur just stood his ground.

'It don't add up,' Monk said finally.

'Maybe it figures,' I said, 'if Frenchy got restless.'

'I'll kill you,' Frenchy said, dropping his hand into his pocket. 'I'll drill you for that, you cheap dick.'

Monk lashed out at him, a quick slap that moved his gunman back on his heels and against the wall, rubbing his jaw with a shaking hand. Monk grabbed his lapels and shook him hard. Once or twice Frenchy's head hit the wall. But he said nothing. Max watched the procedure with his hands folded across his big chest. He stood close to Monk Stang, and when it was all over, Max dragged Frenchy over to the desk and set him down on it. He held Frenchy there.

'Frenchy wouldn't cross me,' Monk said. 'Would you, Frenchy?'

'Listen, how could I?' Frenchy wailed.

'Max was with me all the time.'

'Not all the time,' I suggested. 'Frenchy could have doubled back from Marty's, entered the Brentworth, and knocked off the fat boy. He had plenty of time. That Folsom cluster is worth half a million bucks, Monk. Even your best friend would cross you for a bundle that big.'

They frisked Frenchy. They went over him quickly, emptying his pockets on the floor, unmindful of his squeals of protest. When it was all over, they had found nothing.

'I didn't think he'd do it,' Monk said. 'Frenchy and me, we've been together since we were kids.' He eyed me with a sly and cunning look, as a stirring thought, a theory of his own making, took shape in his mind. 'Who do you think did it, Wells?'

I shook my head. 'That's what the city dicks will be asking, Monk.'

'They'll be asking you, Wells.'

'If they can find me.'

'You're running?' Monk's incredulity knew no bounds.

'I'm running after the killer. I've got a

name and a reputation to keep clean.'

'And when you find the killer?'

'I'll deliver him to the city boys.'

'What for?' Monk smiled slowly. 'The man who knocked off the fat slob has the Folsom cluster, Wells. It could be worth a lot of dough to me.'

'Are you making me an offer?' I asked. 'Save your energy, Monk. If I were you I'd be setting my alibis in order. Because you may have to answer a couple of questions yourself.'

'I know all the answers, Wells.' Monk thumbed his assistants out of the room. He stared at Toni for a long moment and then politely opened the door for her and bowed her into the hall. He closed the door slowly and sat once more behind his desk. He puffed a few drags on a fresh cigar and studied the fresh ash as though he could find the missing gems some- where in the small spark of light. He addressed the cigar. 'I'll pay you ten grand in cash, Wells. No strings. All I want is the inside track when you nab the killer.'

'When and if,' I said.

'You'll do it. I know your reputation.'

'Thanks for nothing,' I said. 'When and if I make the locate on the killer, I do my duty as a citizen, Monk. No deals.'

He shrugged and got up. 'It might be easier for you to do it my way.'

'I've done it the hard way before,' I said.

And then I walked out of there.

12

Izzy Rosen had thousands of friends in an assortment of businesses, each of them willing to favor him with a variety of gestures of goodwill, including less-than-wholesale prices, cut-rate tickets to hit shows, and free entry to every type of sporting event known to man. One of Izzy's intimates owned a small and exclusive hotel on the west side of Central Park: the Rivington, an establishment that catered to the middle-class tourist trade from all over the land.

I took Toni to the Rivington and got her a room.

'Sit tight until you hear from me,' I told her. 'You've got nothing to worry about. There's nothing of yours at the Brentworth, not even a grain of your powder. I cleaned the room thoroughly before we

112

left. When this blows over, you'll get what I promised you.'

'You mean the knockdown to Lawrence Keddy?'

'I mean everything.'

'When will I hear from you?' Toni asked.

We were in her room and it was late at night and she had calmed enough to regain some of her usual aplomb. There was fear in her yet, and it would have been nice to quiet it. But I had things to do. 'I'll be visiting you sooner than you expect,' I said.

'I can't wait, Mike.'

'You'd better. It won't be smart to be seen around town yet. Not until this thing is wrapped up.'

I took a cab to my office, a simple layout in the Cranmer Building, not too far from Grand Central. It was a small place, as exclusive as the men's room in a Turkish bath. A variety of strange businesses occupied the building, including stamp merchants, electrolysis experts and a spattering of minor legal talent too poor to afford the finer suites on Fifth Avenue. But it was home to me. There was an entrance through a short alley, a route I knew well and had used before. It avoided the lobby and led me to the elevator by way of the basement. Here I could move upstairs without checking in on the street level, an arrangement Izzy and I had made a long time ago with Sam, our cordial janitor. He brought the car down at my signal, and greeted me with his accustomed affection.

'You in from Chicago for a while, Mike?' he asked.

'I may be here permanently, and in a city cell, if things don't work out right for me. Anybody looking for me tonight?'

'Nobody but Izzy.'

'He's upstairs?'

'He came in a half-hour ago.'

Izzy was bouncing around in our reception room when I arrived. He leaped my way when my feet crossed the threshold. He grabbed my arm and pushed me back toward the door and flipped off the light switch with his free hand.

'Out,' he said. 'We're taking a quick powder. No questions, yet.'

He told me why on the way down the

fire stairs. He had tried to reach Rico Bruck all afternoon — and failed. This confused and irritated him. He next attempted to phone me at the Brentworth, and again he was foiled. No answer from my room. He assumed that I was engaged in intimate pastimes with Toni and did not want to be disturbed. He waited a reasonable gap of time and phoned again. After that, he became worried. He went at once to the Brentworth.

'The place was lousy with cops,' Izzy said. 'You know why?'

'They discovered the fat boy.'

'You knew all about it?' Izzy halted me on the way out through the alley. 'You didn't butcher him, Mike?'

'Why should I?'

'I'm only asking. I saw Lieutenant Leach down in the lobby of the Brentworth. He said the fat slob's head was kicked in and smashed beyond recognition. I thought maybe you and he got into a squabble. I figured maybe you were cockeyed when you left Marty's and you went back to your room with that fancy broad and found the fat boy waiting for you.'

'And then I kicked his face in? Is that what Leach thinks, Izzy?'

'Leach doesn't exchange theories with me, Mike. You know that. I don't like the smell of it.'

'It stinks,' I said. Then I brought him up to date on the episode with Monk Stang and his hairy henchmen. I retold the whole yarn from the beginning, and Izzy listened without interrupting. We got into a cab and he sat in the corner, gnawing his lip. He would be exploring the details now, running them over in his mental machine, so that we could move quickly — and in the right direction.

I said, 'You worried about Leach, Izzy?'

'He wants you to come in, Mike.'

'Tell him to go to hell,' I said. 'Tell him I'll see him when we've got something.'

'He might get technical — and come after you.'

'Did he say that?'

'Leach will do anything to keep his department looking healthy. The Commissioner has been riding the Midtown boys plenty the last half year. Leach wants arrests — to make his office look busy. He wants you, Mike.'

'What do you think?' I asked. 'If I give myself up now, a couple of the angles I have will die. And I don't want them to die, Izzy. I've got things to do — right away.'

'Then we do them.' Izzy laughed. He snapped out of his trance in a hurry, his mind made up now, anxious to move into action. 'What's our first move, Mike?'

'You've got to make contact with Rico Bruck,' I told him. 'You've got to check him on this deal, Izzy. For my money, he's as ripe a prospect as Monk Stang. I don't trust either of them. Get going, Izzy. We need every minute we can get. When you finish with Rico, go back to the office. I'll phone you there.'

'Where are you headed, Mike?'

'I'm doubling back,' I said. 'I want to see what I can pick up on Sidney Wragge. Who the hell knows his friends and his connections? Maybe he was murdered by an intimate acquaintance. Somebody we never met or knew about might have knocked him off for the Folsom jewels.'

I let him out and told the cabby to take

me downtown. The Kimberly Building was as old as my grandfather, but still retained a gloomy magnificence in the lobby, a broad and well-kept hall with a nest of caged elevators. Sidney Wragge's office was on the twelfth floor, a narrow-halled layout that housed a half-dozen offices. Number 1217 stood at the end of the hall and featured the simple legend:

SIDNEY WRAGGE
Importing — Exporting

The door was open. And the room was a nightmare of upheaval. Every filing cabinet in the tiny place had been emptied on the floor, along with a profusion of books from the small bookshelf behind the desk. The desktop was littered with a variety of papers. Somebody had been through this office with an eye geared for search-and-grab. Every small hiding place had been explored, including the metal petty-cash box, pried open and abandoned on the floor. The rug was white with papers of all sorts — bills and letterheads and correspondence. Even the leather chairs had been overturned and slashed in a frantic quest for the Folsom stones.

I stood flat-footed in the center of the debris, measuring it, frowning at it, snarling at it. I began to examine the desktop, handling everything with a light touch, bending to study every item of importance. I lifted letterheads and billheads, scanning the bits of correspondence quickly. The stuff carried the imprint of a few foreign firms, one The Unique Export, dated in July of last year and bearing the signature of M. Lecleru of Paris, France. The correspondence had to do with the importation of a huge order of trimmings for ladies' hats. The language was forced and stilted.

I ferreted on the floor, comparing the datelines. There were none later than a year ago. The place was probably being used as a front by Wragge, a screen for his book-making operation. I stuffed a few sheets of correspondence in my pockets for future perusal. On my knees, I cased the floor, groping beneath the mounds for anything and everything. I found nothing.

The desk teased me. I swept the top

clean and started through the drawers, searching for the usual small phone list or the little black reference volume, usually found loaded with addresses. I worked my way up to the desktop again, bare now save for the big green blotter and the pen-and-pencil set. The blotter fascinated me. In the lower-right-hand corner, somebody had been doodling, somebody had etched a queer design: *L S — L S — L S*, over and over again, in round letters and in square letters, in fancy curves and curlicues.

Linda Spain?

My mind lit with remembered conversation: the small talk I had made with the druggist's clerk on the corner of Wragge's block. This was a crumb, the first lead, a small and feeble light in the darkness, but enough to move me to action. Linda Spain might be the key to Wragge's intimate life, the link to his background habits, friends, relatives, and personality. Her name sang in my brain, a hopeful lyric, because sometimes the smallest lead can carry an investigator along the high road to success.

So I stood there, as stiff and thoughtful as a two-bit mystic at a county fair. And, standing in the quiet, the little noises of the night came through to me. From somewhere down below the sound of the elevator hummed in the building, a muted buzz but enough to prick my sensibilities. I put out the lights in Sidney Wragge's office. I shook my pants out of there, running along the hall to the fire-stairs door. I slid in behind it and listened, allowing myself a thin crack of vision into the hall.

The elevator stopped and somebody got out. Through the slit, the long corridor was in focus for me, wide enough to observe the two men who advanced toward Wragge's door.

They were Frenchy Armetto and Max.

I started down the stairs. It was time to get out of there.

13

Sidney Wragge's Apartment
12:28 A.M. — July 19th

The way into Sidney Wragge's flat was simple. The buzzers in the hall indicated that he had rooms on the first floor. So I pressed number 6E, the front door clicked open, and I was walking through the broad entrance hall to number 1B, a door on the left side of the building and up front.

And once again, his door was open.

But this time I arrived in time to meet his company. I slipped inside and found myself in a square hall, beyond which lay the small living room. There was a girl standing in there. She almost fell on her face when I walked in.

'Looking for something?' I asked.

She was tall, red-haired, and buxom. Her face was round and pretty, and cut on classic lines. She had large, black eyes.

122

She opened them wide and her broad lipsticked mouth telegraphed her shock. She stepped away from me, back toward the window.

'Who are you?' she asked.

'I asked the first question, lady.'

'What are you doing here?'

'I'll play it again,' I said, and approached her slowly. She flattened herself against the wall near the window. She was dramatic and expressive, without saying a word. She had a figure made to satisfy the customers in any burlesque house, exaggerated in the hips and torso, but the curves were firm and young. She would get high rates in her profession. She kept pushing her hair back from her face in a nervous gesture.

'Are you Linda Spain?'

She nodded dumbly.

'And did you do this job, Linda?'

She stared around her. The place was a cesspool of disorder. It was a two-room apartment, featuring a living-room-sleeping-room combination. The wall-bed had been pulled down and the two pillows lay uncovered, the pillow slips on the floor along with the sheets and blankets. The mattress leaned against the bed at a crazy angle. Around and about it were scattered all the worldly goods of Sidney Wragge, as though some potent wind had blown them there. But no wind short of a hurricane could have wreaked such disorder. Through the arch, the kitchen showed the same treatment. Somebody had emptied the contents of the cupboards on the floor; each small container was opened, a sugar bowl, a few cereal boxes, pots and pans, and a percolator with its innards missing. The lone closet door stood ajar, and Wragge's clothing lay in an untidy heap inside, atop an empty suitcase. There was no need to ferret amid this debris.

'I just got here,' Linda said.

'Just? When?'

'About five minutes before you came.'

She had a voice that shivered its alarm, a girlish soprano that seemed out of place because of her theatrical figure. In the pause, some measure of her personality began to return — the burning brightness of her eyes, the keen and searching quality of her temperament. She was young in the frame but wise in the head, this girl. I came in closer, to hold her away from any show of confidence. She would require handling, toying, playing in a roundabout routine, with no holds barred.

'Where's Sidney?' I asked.

'I don't know, mister. Honest, I don't.'

'You had a date with him here?'

'Who wants to know?'

'Maybe I'm a good friend of his, lady.'

She seemed to shrink further into the wall and her hand went to her pouted mouth. We were close enough for me to count the pores in her face, and it came to me that the dim light in Wragge's room had been hiding her brilliance from me. She was heavily face-painted, her skin aglow with the light tan make-up used on stage. There were lines of heavy pencil around the edges of her eyes, and her eyebrows were hand-drawn and arched too smoothly. She was wearing a low-cut dress, geared for summer comfort but designed for theatrical effect. She was big. She was an Amazonian bump-and-grind queen, a fitting mate for the giant Sidney

Wragge, except for her age.

'I didn't do this, mister,' she pleaded. 'We're old friends, that's all. Look, I have a key to this dump.'

She stepped aside and picked up her bag from the litter on the small desk. Her trembling fingers found the key and she held it up for me, watching my face as I examined it.

'You've been in touch with Sidney today?' I asked.

'I haven't seen him, not yet.'

'And you don't know where he is?'

'Would I be here if I knew?' She was rallying now, slowing down her show of nerves, trying for ease and nonchalance. She added me up slowly, her crimson mouth curving in a gentle smile. She was prettier that way. But her smile couldn't wipe away the trouble in her eyes, the edge of worry that no display of humor could kill.

'You're not a cop,' she said. 'Are you, big boy?'

'Suppose I'm not?'

'I'd feel a lot better.'

'Where would that get me?'

'It all depends where you want to go.'

There was the sound of a door opening from somewhere through a few walls. She froze as she listened to it. She began to tremble again and moved close to me, putting a cold hand on mine.

'Listen, will you help me?'

'Try me. I'm a Boy Scout at heart, especially with big girls like you.'

'I'm afraid,' Linda said. 'I've been scared silly for the past hour or so.'

'Afraid of what?'

'A man. Ever since I did my closing number at the show, there's a jerk been following me. After the show, two of my pals and me went out for coffee. That was when I had the feeling this mug was watching me. He was in a dogcart, and he looked in through the window once. Then he came back again.'

'How do you know he was looking at you?'

She shivered violently. 'I started for home in a cab. He got into one behind me and started to follow me. I begged my cabby to try to lose him. Lucky for me, he was a nice cabby. He drove fast and managed to shake the guy. Then I came here. I wanted Sidney to help me, to take me home and stay with me.'

She was talking fast and talking smoothly, out of her obvious driving fear. She paused only once, to jerk her head toward the window when a passing car hissed by.

'Why didn't you go to the cops?' I asked.

She eyed me with discouragement. 'You ever been to the Braddock, big boy?'

'What's the Braddock got to do with it?'

'Come down some night. The show we put on in that dump is only for the private trade. The Braddock's been closed since the Minsky wheel died in New York. We run a strictly stag deal, with tickets on sale only under hats. What we give the boys in that place is so hot that the cops would put the lid on it, and send some of us away where we couldn't shake our cans for a while. So how could I go to the cops?'

'Who was the jerk who followed you?'

'I don't know.'

'What did he look like?'

'I never saw him before in my life. It's hard to remember.' She rubbed her brow and scowled at her inefficient memory. 'Oh, it's happened before, a couple of times, nuts in the audience who get ideas about the girls in the line. They're different, though. They come up to you at the stage door and proposition you, and after you turn them down, maybe they'll try again. But those characters are open. You tell them you'll call a cop — and they fade. This guy was something different. He was a sneak. He didn't give me a chance to get a good gander at his face. He scared me silly. If you're a real friend of Sidney's, please take me home?'

It was after one in the morning and she was begging me to take her home. If I played along with her, I might learn something useful. So I let her continue her urgent plea. I listened to her and played hard to get. She talked on and on in an unbridled tempo. She was nervous and upset, but all of it was genuine. She sold me a bill of goods, and when I softened her eyes told me that she would pay off later, in dividends that I could understand.

We left Sidney Wragge's and walked to the corner. Her arm was tight in mine and she hugged me eagerly, as though I might sprint away from her if she released me. The streets were dead, and the city slept and snored with only the dull hum of its breathing coming through to us, the rumbles and roars of the muted traffic. Our cab entered the theatrical district and turned to the East Side. Nobody followed us.

14

Second Avenue
1:47 A.M. — July 19th

She had me stop the cab on Second Avenue, so that she could try a neighborhood bar for a bottle of bourbon. I let the cabby go and we walked a block to a dimly lit joint where Linda was sure we could get what she wanted. She came out with a bottle of good stuff.

She patted it fondly and said, 'We can use this tonight, huh?'

And she led me into a side street, as quiet and dead as the inside of a library. It was a short walk from the corner to her apartment house, but almost as soon as we made the turn, my short hairs went up. Were we being followed? Somebody moved behind us on clever legs, spryly and with an experienced step, soft and effortless. I didn't turn. I pressed her arm and she came closer.

'Pull up short when we get inside the lobby,' I whispered, holding my head in its normal position for intimate talk. 'There's somebody behind us.'

I felt her stiffen as we finished the last few steps to the door. It was a small apartment house, of the same type as Sidney Wragge's, but on a slightly higher level in the social stratum. It was newer and more dignified, with an entrance that featured a marble fish spewing water into a green and brackish pond. A few tired goldfish swam around under some floating lettuce.

I pulled Linda behind the abutment of the hall wall. I held her there. Time ticked by. A minute? And then the figure of a man appeared against the frosted window of the entrance door. He was little and he seemed stooped as he leaned into the door and pushed it slowly open. I let him come four steps our way. And then I made a grab for him.

He pulled to one side with an animal's reaction to a sudden tormentor, spry and with electric speed. But I had a hand on his shoulder and jerked so hard that I almost wrenched the jacket off him, complete with shoulder pads. The hall was lit only by the reflected glow of an interior fixture, but I could see enough to catch the terror in his face. I started my right hand up toward his chin when Linda ran toward me and clung to me. Her voice carried a shaking urgency.

'Jesus, no!' she begged. 'That's only Champ.'

'Who the hell is this gorilla?' the little man whined.

I released him, almost overcome by internal merriment at the picture he made. 'Champ of what?' I asked.

'He's Champ Crowley,' Linda said. 'He lives upstairs — a neighbor of mine, big boy.'

Champ Crowley adjusted his haberdashery with a wriggling and squirming display of petulance. He was an overgrown midget, wrinkled in the neck and face, an ex-jockey I remembered out of the *Racing Form* days of my youth. We shook hands and he accepted my apology with good grace. He led us up to the second-floor landing, where he invited us into his nest for a nightcap. He had Apartment 2B, directly across the hall from Linda.

Champ broke out some glasses and did his best to make us comfortable. He spoke with a nasal twang, a hillbilly diction that made his citified slang seem incongruous.

'Friend of Sidney's,' Linda explained, smiling my way.

'Any friend of Sid's is a friend of mine,' said Champ. 'When's he getting back, you know?'

'He's back,' I said. 'He's in town.'

'A good boy, Sid.'

'One of the best. You know him long?'

'Long?' The little jockey scratched his stubbled chin and reflected. 'How long would you say, Linda?'

'Maybe three, four months?'

'That's about it,' Champ agreed, creasing his face with a wise grin that brought more wrinkles out around his eyes. At his ease and with a liquor glass in his hand, he looked like a boy of twelve playacting at being grown-up. 'I guess I first met Sid about two months ago.'

Linda was edging close to me at the table, and in the conversational lag, Champ Crowley gave her a slow wink, and a small part of his wit.

'You don't expect Sid any more tonight, Linda?' he asked.

'He could come.'

'But you don't want him knocking at your door?'

'You're my boy, Champ.' She blew him a kiss, gulped the dregs of her drink and squeezed my arm purposefully. 'Champ don't fall asleep until maybe the sun is coming up. He's an A-1 watchdog for me, once in a while, hah, Champ?'

I dawdled with my drink. What was happening here tickled my curiosity and glued me to my chair. This kind of talk could open the door to Sidney Wragge for me, laying bare the personal pattern of his life, the intimate day-to-day revelations that could stack up well for me in the summing-up. What he meant to Linda Spain interested me. She was leaning in to me and nuzzling her pretty face against mine. But the horseplay didn't seem to disturb Champ at all. Had he seen it before? My mind struggled for a clear and well-imagined picture of the fat man in a situation like this. The zany tableau: the projection of Sidney Wragge into this room, into these circumstances, among these people — all these things combined to evoke laughter. He would be funny here, that was it. He would be a ponderous, elegant, dignified tub of lard, out slumming with his ten-cent lady love, visiting a bony midget. My memory of Champ Crowley included a headline story of a jockey who was involved in a fix. A long time ago. Ten years? Fifteen years? And after that, it came to me that Champ had gained some notoriety as a bookie, an upper-crust tout with a list of clients among the socially elite. And what did Sidney Wragge have to do with this intelligent midget? And how often did he come to wrestle with his amour, the Amazonian Linda Spain?

The conversational bout was stimulating her jittery restlessness, so that she gave me her liquored eyes, laying her message on the line. And through all of this, Champ Crowley only sat and slurped his drink, his eyes half-closed, his mouth alive with a knowing smile, as though the routine was something he had seen before, over and over again.

Linda stood up, tugged me to my feet, and escorted me to the door.

15

Linda Spain's Apartment
2:43 A.M. — July 19th

Linda's rooms were decorated in the harum-scarum pattern of showgirl existence, a combination of furniture-styling and upholstered lavishness that betrayed her profession. The small living room was jam-packed with a variety of cheap stuff, including a couch that was broad enough to accommodate a visiting ball club, complete with the manager and bat boy. It was a velvety monstrosity, dominating the room, with cushions out of some nightmare of a Turkish harem.

A huge chromo hung over the couch, a picture of bright and lavish nonsense that caught your eye and held it. It was a landscape, an original, done by a painter who should have limited his activities to brushwork on garages. It was bad. It was corn. But the sight of a work of art, however bad, seemed out of place in such a living room.

'You like my oil painting?' Linda asked, joining me as I squinted at it. 'Pretty, isn't it?'

'The best,' I said.

'Sidney gave it to me.'

'He's got a great eye for art. I'll bet a picture like this is worth a lot of loot.'

'You think so?' She eyed the chromo curiously, as though she had just seen it for the first time. 'How much?'

'Hard to say. Where'd Sid get it?'

'An auction place up on Sixth Avenue. Sidney's a sucker for those clip joints. I'll bet he paid plenty for this thing. I'll bet he paid maybe a couple of hundred.'

'At least,' I agreed. 'I didn't know Sid was an art lover.'

'Poo,' said Linda. She waltzed over to a small table and showed me a small Chinese incense burner, complete with grinning figurine and a square receptacle for the smoldering junk. It was a masterpiece of brass and filigreed carving, the sort of trinket the sucker tourists fall for on their trips to Chinatown. 'Look at this. More junk from the auction dumps.'

She retired to her bedroom and I busied myself with the fresh bottle of bourbon. Her windows faced the rear of the house, overlooking a broad court now black with gloom. I pulled the drapes and squatted on the horrible couch, dosing myself with two large slugs of liquor. She came back wearing a robe of shining silk, pulled tight against the lines of her voluptuous figure. Her red hair was combed out and fell in graceful swoops over her shoulders, long and almost as colorful as her costume. She sat alongside me.

'I feel like a heel,' I said. 'Sid wouldn't like this. He's out on a tough deal.'

'What tough deal could Sid be out on?'

'Monk Stang.'

'Who the hell is Monk Stang?' She asked the question easily, frowning at it, her eyes half-closed.

'You mean to say that Sid never mentioned Monk to you?' I asked.

'When Sid comes to see me, he doesn't waste too much time gabbing.'

'Maybe I don't blame him.'

'Stop talking, lover boy. Forget about Sid, huh?'

'You're making it easy.'

'I'll make it easier,' she said, and set about proving it. Her lips were warm and sweet. She treated me to a long taste of them. 'You feel better now?'

'Feeling no pain, Linda. No wonder Sid talks about you so much.'

'He does? What does he say?'

'He's nuts about you.'

She leaned away from me and studied me for a short interlude. She was drunk, but she was thoughtful. 'What's the idea of your big pitch for Sid?' she asked. 'The way you talk, maybe you're his brother or something.'

'We're good friends, that's all.'

'You want to tell him something for me?' she asked. 'Something special? Listen. Tell him to stop with the serious routine. I got other friends, you understand? In my business, a dame does funny things — crazy, maybe, but that's the way I like it. I see a guy like you and he does me a favor — why, I want to pay off for him. I do what I like, and when I like it.

But that don't mean I have to marry the lug I'm wrestling, does it now?'

From somewhere in another county, a church bell bonged once, a brassy, hollowing ring that died slowly in the summer air over the city. Two-thirty? Three? How could I fiddle with time? She was near me, close enough that her bodily fragrance became an overpowering command, a deep and penetrating summons to my animal instincts.

16

Linda Spain's Apartment
4:45 A.M. — July 19th

I slept with a jittery restlessness. In the blackness of the first deep pit of slumber, Linda left me. The studio couch sagged and lifted as she eased her weight away from me. After that, there was the vague and foggy tinkle of glass and running water from somewhere beyond her bedroom. Sleep won me, finally. But my mind still seemed to boil with disquiet, filling my rest with nightmare images drawn from my hectic hours during the past day. Impulse told me to be up and away. I had neglected Izzy, failing to call him as I promised. He would be wondering about me. I dreamed of his trip to Rico Bruck, and built a fantasy out of his interview with the skillful little gangster. What had happened? The little bells in my conscience rang a tune in my subconscious, stirring me, irritating me, biting at the strings of sleep that bound me to the couch in Linda Spain's living room.

But Morpheus had stunned me. I was dead to the world, sunk deep into the cushion of fatigue, against which my will could not stir me. I rolled and pitched myself awake. I made the gateway to consciousness the hard way by slamming my head against the wooden arm of the couch, so that I arose in a hurry.

I was wide awake and sitting up. The room still seemed unreal and vague, like a part of the fogged and gossamer background of my recent dreams. But reality came to me quickly. There was gray light filtering through the courtyard window. My watch told me it was almost six. I had been dead to the world for over two hours.

Something stirred. Behind me? In the next room? I rubbed at my eyes and sat there, as wooden as a stiff in the morgue, feeling my spine go cold with the prickles of tension. There was a dull and padded sound from somewhere close by, a noise that was not a noise. A padded footfall? A body in motion? Linda? And was she awake and coming toward me through the door behind my back?

I shifted my weight, and a fickle spring sang a whining tune beneath me from the bowels of the couch upholstery. And then I tried to turn, but it was too late.

Somebody hit me. It was a flat clap of pain, high behind my ear, a lightning crash that caught me off-balance and brought strange music to my inner ear, an offbeat twang in a shrieking flood of noise, a vicious chord complete with twisting bands of sharpening light. The hammers of hell banged in my brain. The stabbing pricks of a thousand needles lit at my head and I began to fall to one side, off the couch and onto the floor and through the rug into the black hole of sleep from which I had just come. I struggled against the blow, but my eyes were blinded, shut tight in the reflex spasm of dizziness that was carrying me away from the bastard who hit me.

Then I was out for good, as stiff and dead as a plucked duck.

* * *

The sun was a straight and narrow beam of light aimed at my eyes through the window on the court. It burned into me. I clawed up at it and rolled away from it, and in the process of shifting my body, the spark of life was revived in me and I came awake.

My head pounded and bounced. It took time to bring the room back into focus, long enough for the little band of sunlight to move a few inches away from me. I lay on my side and watched it travel, losing myself in the perspective of rug and desk, on the far wall.

'Linda!' I yapped, and rested after the feeble shout.

There was no answer from the bedroom. Was it Linda Spain who had slugged me? I shouted again, stronger this time. I pushed my body up and grabbed a chair and struggled to sit. I made it after the third try. The noises of the city came through to me, slowly. There was traffic moving outside in the busy street. From across the courtyard a cacophony of off-key music spread itself around me, somebody practicing the piano and doing a very bad job of it. The sound of dishes and pots and pans came through the wall across the room. My nose picked up the smell of bacon and coffee. My eyes rolled to the window again. The window was open.

I dragged myself up, and let my muscles grab hold of my legs and keep me standing. I crossed the room and stood at the window, staring out at the fire escape and letting my brain oil itself into action again. Had somebody come in through this window while I slept? The window hadn't been open when Linda and I were wrestling on the couch.

My head, above the right ear, was wet with blood. The touch of my tentative fingers on the wound set off a skittering rush of pain; enough to make me yell out. I looked at myself in the mirror. Whoever hit me had tried for the jackpot. The blood stained my cheek and neck. I stifled the impulse to upchuck. I got away from that mirror in a hurry and ran into Linda Spain's bedroom.

In the dim light I saw her on the bed in an attitude of blissful slumber, her well-rounded body relaxed on the coverlet. She slept in a delightful pose, her arms outstretched as though welcoming her long lost love, her long and beautiful legs crossed. Her wealth of red hair swept down over her shoulders. She was as naked as a stag reel. I stepped forward to wake her.

And then my knees jellied. And I stared down at her and listened to my heart pump blood into my head, my eyes riveted on the right side of her tantalizing torso. Somebody had ruined forever the graceful lusciousness of the Amazonian beauty. Somebody had stabbed her as she slept. Her chest was lacerated with gore, an ugly wound that dug at my eyes.

Linda Spain was dead.

I stepped away from her, weak and soft in the head now, overcome by the fresh surge of sickness that clawed at my gut. I ran for the bathroom.

I made it just in time.

17

'You feeling better?' Izzy asked. 'Or do you want me to get a doctor?'

'I'll survive,' I said, and adjusted the adhesive over my ear.

He was frying another pair of eggs for me in his kitchenette. The coffee was hot and good and I gulped it thirstily. It was only eight, but Izzy had not slept well all night, holding the door open for my arrival. He was dozing in his easy chair when I walked in, but the sight of my bloody head had made him bounce with his accustomed vigor, tending my wound with the skill of a practised medico. He asked me no questions while mopping me up. He muttered an esoteric curse when it was time for the bandaging, light-fingering the tape in place with nimble hands.

Now he joined me at the table and waited for me to spill. I spilled for him.

'Crazier and crazier,' Izzy commented, after I had put a period to my personal account. 'Your hunch must have been right, Mike. Sidney Wragge was a personality, a man with many enemies. One of them guessed the set-up; one of them figured Linda Spain had the Folsom cluster.'

'The man who followed her?'

'Who else?'

'It doesn't make sense, Izzy. I had a long talk with her. She didn't seem to know anything about her fat boyfriend. She also didn't want any part of him.'

'That wouldn't prevent Fatso from letting her hold the gems for a while, would it?'

'He'd have to be a lunkhead to trust her. She might have been playing Sidney for the number-one sucker on her list. But I can't see him falling for her line of chatter. She was a lightweight mentally, with none of the subtleties a man like Wragge would demand in a dame. He hit me as being a pretty hep guy, complete with an Oxford-type accent straight out of a British movie. Why would a cosmopolite trust a two-bit shimmy queen?'

'Cosmopolite, shmosmopolite,' said Izzy. 'Love is a kick in the slats, Mike.'

'Not for Sidney Wragge, it wouldn't be,' I insisted. 'He was too dignified for that kind of horseplay.'

Izzy leaned over and poked me in the ribs, slyly. 'And you, Mister Smartboy? How about you? Didn't you just admit she conned you into a session on the couch? If she was clever enough to sidetrack you from your business, she could have been just the gal to land a fat fish like Sidney Wragge. Nobody loves a fat man, remember? And when a big and lusty piece like Linda Spain makes a pass at a heavyweight, who's to say he wouldn't fall for her like a tub of lard? She could have talked him into believing he was the big flame in her life. She could have worked him around to going soft in the head, the way you describe her. For my money, it happened that way.'

'You think she had the Folsom stones?'

'Why not? Maybe Wragge hid them in

151

her flat and told her to sit on them for a while.' Izzy warmed to his theory, abandoning his coffee while he outlined his brainstorm. 'If he was going to double-cross Monk Stang, her apartment would be a good hiding place, no? He might have met her during the day yesterday, slipped her the gems and told her to stash them away. Now, just suppose that Frenchy Armetto happened to be on Wragge's tail when the gems were passed. What would Frenchy do? You guessed it. He'd wait for her and follow her home after the show, wouldn't he? He would be the man who watched her from the dogcart. He followed you when you escorted her home. He waited until he figured you were asleep. Then he came in by way of the fire escape, knifed her, and returned to the living room to crack you. A deal like that would add up, Mike. The cops would find you conked and bleeding and assume that you and the girl had a lovers' quarrel, after which you knifed her and returned to sleep off your drink. Period.'

'Question mark,' I added. 'A big

question mark, Izzy. You're basing your entire pitch on the fact that Sidney Wragge put his trust in Linda. I can't buy it.'

'You got any better ideas?'

He had me there. It could have been the hammering in my head that had damned my mental flow. It could have been the empty anger that boiled my stomach and cut me away from any successful reasoning at this hour of the morning. I knew only that I was filling with a gnawing impatience, a restlessness that would wear me out soon.

Izzy understood my mood. He let me pace the floor, and I threw him a few questions about Rico Bruck and yesterday evening. He had made contact with Rico, finally, in his suite at the Waldorf. He had quizzed Bruck and Gilligan for a full hour, running over the account of their activities from the time their plane landed at LaGuardia. But they were shocked and puzzled to hear of the fat man's murder. They had alibied themselves across the board. Gilligan and Bruck had visited a few clubs, because Rico intended to buy a new bistro in town and set up his first New York outfit.

'I checked their stories,' Izzy said. 'It took time, but I reached all of their contacts. They visited three nightclubs — one in Greenwich Village and two uptown. The club owners had set dates for Rico and backed him up. He and Gilligan were out shopping, all right.'

'They bought those alibis!' I yelped. 'You don't really go for their routine, Izzy?'

'I checked it, Mike.'

'Who were the club owners they visited?'

'Three crumbs, of course,' Izzy admitted sadly. 'Three heels you could buy off for buttons, naturally. But also three characters who would stand up and scream for Rico because they're all dirty, as dirty as Bruck. Still, what Rico says he's got, he's got. And how are you going to prove he maybe butchered the fat boy?'

'Rico Bruck wouldn't butcher a dying beetle,' I said, remembering his history. 'And neither would Gilligan. Anybody else come in with them from Chicago?'

'You think Rico brought in some of his boys?'

'I wouldn't put it past him,' I said, and started for the door.

'Where are you going, Mike?'

'Up to the Waldorf to ask Rico a few questions.'

'Wait for me,' said Izzy, and grabbed his coat and hat.

18

Rico Bruck had a high and airy suite at the Waldorf, one of the finest in the tower. I leaned on his bell and waited for him. We were waking him early, and I enjoyed the chore. The bell rang for a full five minutes before the door opened a crack and a voice that was not Rico's inquired, 'What the hell do you want?' A gruff and sleepy monotone, half-whisper, half-sand.

I pushed hard at the door and felt it slam up against flesh, after which the whisper became a shout, and I moved inside to face a familiar ape.

It was Elmo, the big doorman from the Card Club. He held his nose and reached out for me with a hairy paw. I slapped it down and sidestepped him. He growled an indecent word at me and his pig eyes struggled for some decision in the crisis.

156

He stepped back toward the living room, working his huge arms in the gestures of a wrestler preparing for the lunge.

I said, 'Forget it, Elmo. Go wake the boss.'

'You know this gorilla?' Izzy asked.

'Elmo and I are old pals. Aren't we, Elmo?'

'Out,' said Elmo, working his jaws into an impressive mask of menace. 'Scram. Before I get sore and slap you around.'

Izzy stepped between us and tapped the big man on the chest, a quick movement that surprised Elmo and threw him off-guard for an important instant. 'Do what the man says, Elmo. And do it fast, or else I'll have to take you down to see a man. Downtown. And the man is a nasty policeman, who'll ask you questions about where you were yesterday. You got the answers ready, Elmo? Or do you want to talk them over with Rico?'

Sometimes a mouse can give an elephant pause. The leathery jaw of the giant dropped open, revealing an impressive array of gold in the uppers. Something a little stronger than surprise came to life on the iron face, a mixture of fear and doubt. Elmo had a tic, high up on his left cheek, close to the eye. The muscle began its rhumba bump, and Elmo stepped backward slowly, retreating before Izzy Rosen's belligerent purpose.

Then Rico came in. He appeared through the door on the right, tying a knot in his sash and adjusting it on his spare frame. He was bedecked in splendor, a dark blue silk robe, with the initials *R.B.* in gold embroidery, small enough to be seen over on Madison Avenue. We had tugged him from between the sheets. He repressed a yawn and stepped jauntily into the room.

'Wells,' he said. 'It's about time you showed.'

'Where's Gilligan?' I asked.

'Gilligan stays at his own dump — the Brentworth.'

'Get him.'

'What for? I don't need him.'

'You may need a lawyer,' I told him, 'sooner than you expect.'

'Forget it,' Rico said easily. He lifted the phone and began to order breakfast, inviting us to join him and ordering an extra pot of coffee even after we refused. He stared up and said, 'Who hit you, Wells? Anybody I know?'

'You took the words right out of my mouth, Rico. Who hit me?'

I was looking at Elmo. He stood behind Rico, legs spread in the posture he used at the door of the Card Club. He licked his lip and glared at me. My words bounced off him. He was as emotional as a chimpanzee listening to a recital of Shakespeare. Rico turned his way and the ape eyes only flicked at his boss for a breath of time. But there was nothing in them, nothing at all.

'You're wondering about Elmo?' Rico inquired.

'He wasn't in your little act last night,' Izzy said.

'Elmo was with me ever since we got here.'

'Can you prove it?'

'What the hell for?' Rico said testily. His face was sallow and half-asleep. He needed a shave badly. He looked tired and weak, a little man with a big worry. He lit a cigar and sucked at it for a minute, allowing it to quiet his inner man. He turned my way and shook his head at me, almost apologetically. 'Listen, Wells, I don't blame you for flipping your wig. You got every reason in the world for giving me a bad time. But you're wrong about the deal. You're dead wrong.'

'Am I?'

Elmo said, 'I can prove I was with Rico.'

'*Shut up!*' Rico barked.

'Why not let the man talk?' Izzy asked. 'Go ahead, Elmo. Tell us.'

Elmo held back, staring at his master with the eyes of a mastiff who awaits a trainer's command. What he saw gave him pause. He blinked his optics and swallowed hard and lapsed into his former state of animation, as mobile as a stone in a quarry and twice as emotional.

'Listen to me, Wells,' Rico said. 'Listen and think. You know the score on this deal, if you use your head. I called you in to tail the fat slob to New York. Why did I do this? You remember why? It was because somebody phoned me in Chicago and told me the bastard was carrying the Folsom cluster to a New York fence. And who sent him to New York? There's only one hood on earth who could have engineered that Folsom heist. That man is Monk Stang. Now, follow me. Follow me close. Who would rub out the fat man? Monk, of course. Monk had one of his boys tail the fat man to your hotel room. Frenchy Armetto, maybe. Or maybe Max. It fits that way.'

'It could fit in other ways,' Izzy said.

'Never,' said Rico.

'You could have done the job.'

'Kill it,' Rico almost shouted, grinding out his cigar with a vicious gesture. 'I told you where I was all day yesterday, Rosen. I can prove it.'

'Half a million bucks is a load of loot,' Izzy said quietly. 'Even for you, it's big money, Rico. Big enough to invent fairy tales.'

Rico got up quickly and lunged for Izzy. But I was alongside him in time to grab the little punk and freeze him in his tracks. I jerked him up short, holding him hard and tight, pulling his fancy lapels up until his head stuck out like a turtle on a log. I tugged the robe tight around him and shook him. Elmo was coming toward us. I lifted Rico and threw him at his gorilla. They bumped. Hard. Hard enough to knock the breath out of Rico Bruck.

He fell forward and grabbed the back of the nearest chair. Elmo was passing him, but Rico held out a hand and waved him to a quick stop. Then Rico coughed, a high and raspy fit of breathlessness. He straightened and adjusted his robe and stared at me wearily.

'All right, Wells,' he almost whispered. 'Let it pass. Because I don't blame you, like I said. You got every reason for slapping me around. You see, I understand. But you're wrong. You're all wrong. I put you on a job because I trusted you. Listen, if you still think I bumped off the fat boy, I'll make you another deal. I'll prove I'm right and you're wrong. If I bumped off the fat boy, I've got the Folsom cluster, right?'

'Right.'

'But I haven't got it. So I'll pay you off if you find it for me, understand? Whoever bumped Fatso has the stones, right? You find me the murderer and I pay you ten grand.' He let himself slide back into a chair. 'Now do you believe me?'

The door to the hall opened and John Gilligan came in, followed by a boy with a wagonload of breakfast. Gilligan almost ran across the room to his client, bending over him with the worried look of a father over an injured brat. There was something off-key in his solicitude. Gilligan was out of character with this slipping from his dignified routine for such obvious buttering-up of Rico. It was well known in Chicago that Gilligan earned a fat retainer from the little gambler. But the tableau didn't make sense. Izzy tossed me an appreciative wink.

'What's happened?' Gilligan asked us angrily. He did not move from Rico's side.

'Rico will break it down for you,' I told him, and started for the door, followed by Izzy. I paused in the hall to look back at the scene behind me. Gilligan was frozen in his pose, with one arm on Rico's shoulder. Bruck only stared at us weakly and pushed himself to his feet.

'Remember what I told you, Wells,' he

said. 'Ten grand for the murderer.'

'What are you saying, Rico?' Gilligan asked, his regal voice hushed and tight with anxiety. 'What's the deal?'

'Wells knows what I'm talking about.'

'Wait a minute, Wells.'

But we were out in the hall before he finished his oily dialogue. And I slammed the door in his face.

19

We split the freight on the deal, Izzy and I. We broke apart and channeled our efforts into different streams, the loose ends in the life of Sidney Wragge. We chewed it over a slow lunch, because it was a challenge and a gut-ache to both of us. Especially me. A private investigator should know his way around the dead ends. A working shamus is reluctant to play the role of patsy, fall guy, or just plain dope. My head ached with an itch of angry frustration because of the incident in Linda Spain's nest, because of the smell of my assailant, the sneaking crumb who had slashed her lovely torso. The skulking horror in her bedroom filled me with a fit of heaves, a budding sympathy for the girl who was Linda Spain. She was outside the stinking mess

165

for me. Her honest monologue about her morals and the life she led, her frank and open pitch for me — all these things closed her away from any guilt or involvement in the strange story of Sidney Wragge. And, thinking of Linda Spain, I knew that I would never rest until the pieces of the puzzle were set in place.

Izzy went off to pick up what he could at the Kimberly Building.

A lead is a lead. I thumbed through the phone book list of auction emporiums on Sixth Avenue, finding only one in the uptown area. A cab deposited me before a small and evil-smelling dump, loaded with a variety of junk brought there from the odds and ends of the storage warehouse overflow. The window was dirty with dust. A galaxy of assorted oil daubs lined the glass, paintings of sheep in mangers, dead fish and lobsters, plus the usual tripe in academic landscaping. I had more than a casual interest in the art section. Once, long ago, when my caricaturing was a prime ambition, I had deluded myself with dreams of an attic and a painting career. There was nothing much left of the old drive now, but the love of fine art still remained alive in me. I stood outside the auction room for a long pause, studying the types of pictures sold here. It might well be the place where Sidney Wragge had purchased his gift for Linda Spain.

A swarthy gnome in a filthy apron emerged from the shadows in the rear of the place when I entered.

'The boss,' I said. 'He in?'

'You're talking to him, mister.' He squinted at me in the gloom, rolling his head for a better view of me in the quick and efficient appraisal of the master salesman. 'Anything I can do?'

'A picture. I want to buy an oil picture.'

'Excellent. I got some good stuff back here.'

He led me through narrow corridors of stacked furniture, frames, bric-a-brac, metallic ornaments, and lamps. The way to the art section was devious but purposeful, a roundabout tour through the stock so that I might see something I admired on the way. I admired nothing. There was a long window facing the yard in the rear. Against the sill, art blossomed in a hundred canvases, running the gamut from starchy nudes to muddy marines, complete with four-masted schooners.

'Now,' said the merchant, 'just what kind of a painting you want, mister?'

'Landscapes. I like landscapes.'

'Landscapes with animals?'

'Landscapes with trees.'

'Only trees?' he asked. 'I got better ones with animals, sheep and cows, also with buildings. Farmhouses, like.'

'Trees,' I insisted. Sometimes a painter specializes in one type of chromo. The man who had created the daub in Linda Spain's living room was only a semi-pro. It could be that his entire stock had been found in some dusty corner of a warehouse. In that case, the auctioneer might handle the whole inventory of his work. He would be easy to recognize. I remembered his dirty browns and vivid greens, the color of sick and dying vegetation, the hallmark of the amateur who yearns to paint foliage with some degree of naturalism. Such handling of paint would be easy to spot.

We started through the stock. The little man sweated as he displayed his wares, holding each up to the light from his yard and making small clucking noises of appreciation as he tried to sell me his enthusiasm. For over a half hour he toiled for me. Then he faced me wearily, mopped his brow and shook his head sadly.

'Listen, mister, what do you want? Leonardo da Vinci, maybe, for my prices?'

'I'll know it when I see it.'

'Look for yourself,' he said. 'I'm too old for such pastimes.'

I looked. He left me to my pleasure, answering the brassy bell at the front of the store. I flipped through the paintings carefully, studying each for some clue to the artist I wanted. There was a series of marines after a while, primitive boats on primitive oceans. The green of the waves held me. Was this the same artist? And then I hit a painting of a shoreline, with the trees bending over a blue lagoon. I was home.

The picture featured a frame out of the last century, as gaudy and fussy as an old maid's bib. And all the other paintings by the same man were enclosed in the same antique type of frame. I studied the brush strokes and concentrated on the color. The foliage and grass sang with overtones of nausea, the same sticky treatment as the chromo in Linda Spain's flat. I whistled the proprietor back to me.

'This is for me,' I said, showing my delight by cocking my eye at it under the light.

'A nice job,' he agreed. 'Good painting.'

'Funny that the artist didn't sign his name. It can't be worth much.'

'Lots of good artists don't sign their work,' argued the owner. 'Like when they do sketches and stuff like this. But that don't mean the sketches aren't worth money. Not at all.'

'How much for this one?'

'For you — fifty dollars.'

'That's too much,' I said thoughtfully rubbing my nose and stepping back to squint and peer at it through half-closed eyes. 'Still, maybe it matches. Maybe it's like the one Sidney bought.'

'You have somebody with another one?'

170

'A friend of mine told me he bought one like this,' I explained. 'I want to get an extra one to surprise him, you understand. But Sidney's painting didn't have a frame like this.' I put the painting on the sill and gave it another dose of slow scrutiny. 'I've got to make sure this is the place where Sidney got his.'

'Sidney who? Maybe I'll remember.'

'Wragge,' I said. 'Sidney Wragge, a very fat man.'

'Of course,' the owner said without pause, snapping his dirty fingers. 'I remember the man. Sold him one maybe a month or so ago. It's a good thing you mentioned he was fat. A fat man, you can't forget so easy, right? I even remember the picture — a landscape, it was. Also, I put a different frame on for your friend. The whole deal was sixty-five dollars. I'll do the same for you.'

'You say you framed the picture for him? Have you got a record of the sale in your files?'

'Record?' he exploded, throwing out his hands in a gesture of frustration. 'Who keeps such records? What do you want records for? You don't believe me? You don't believe I sold your friend a picture? Listen, I just happened to have a frame around that looked better on the picture, so I threw it in. A store like this, we don't keep such records. Sixty-five bucks was the deal, like I said.' He watched me for some reaction to his powerful sales drive. I continued to thumb my chin and look doubtful. And then the spark of a fresh and convincing light flooded his tired eyes. 'Look,' he spouted, 'I'll prove I know your fat friend, even if I don't know his name. You go to him and ask him, didn't he buy a Chinese incense burner here? That, my friend, will settle it.'

Sidney Wragge had bought the picture here, along with the Chinese monstrosity. But the deal set off a thousand doubts in my hammering head. Good taste is an obvious possession sometimes. Taste will come through in a man's personality by way of a hundred signals in his normal behavior. Sidney Wragge talked like an Oxford professor. Sidney Wragge dressed in the dignified pattern of a man of discernment. He had conducted himself with the calm and controlled gestures of an upper-crust gentleman. Why, then, would he stoop to the purchase of such baubles, such obvious gewgaws? Was it because of his great love for Linda Spain that he suddenly forgot his breeding? Could it be possible that he deliberately bought this tripe to please her? The business of the changed frame suggested that Wragge might have tried to improve the effect of the chromo by surrounding it with something more modern in the way of a framing job. But nothing on earth can alter the effect of a really bad painting. Sidney Wragge would know this, yet he had paid fifteen dollars extra for the new frame.

I said, 'Did my friend ask for the new frame?'

'Ask? I sold him a new one because the old one was too cracked, too beat-up.'

'You've been a great help,' I told the little merchant, and held out a ten-dollar bill for him to admire. 'This is for you, my friend.'

'But I haven't sold you anything yet,' he said, amazed.

173

'You've sold me plenty.'

I left him shaking his head and beaming at me, and then staring at the money in befuddlement. He had merchandised only a small and challenging idea, but the thought was well worth the investment. I filed the idea away in my cluttered brain and walked quickly out of his den of discards.

20

Champ Crowley's Apartment
4:35 P.M. — July 19th

Champ Crowley sat alone in his living room. Leach's boys had left a half-hour before my arrival, and the little jockey was in no mood for further patter. His pasty face was a shade lighter than the pea-green lamp alongside his chair. He jabbed a fresh cigarette in his mouth and lit it nervously. He gave me his intimate opinion of the guardians of the law in two-syllable words, none of which could be found in Webster's unabridged catalogue of lexicography.

'Leach!' he spat. 'A good name for the crumb, isn't it? He's got a long nose — too long for his own good — for my dough. I don't mind answering their halfwit questions about last night. I told them all I knew, and I told it to them straight. But have they any right to try to break me down about my racket? I ask you, where do they come off grilling me about making book?'

Champ showed his softening mood by dragging out a bottle and sharing it with me. I had an angle to explore with him. I had a pitch, and I was thankful that I could still sell myself to him as 'Art Seton,' an out-of-town friend of Sidney Wragge. Izzy's suggestion for keeping Wragge's death out of the public press might pay off for me here. Champ Crowley could be made to talk about Sidney, if he thought Wragge still lived and breathed. He would clam up and go sour if he knew the truth. Right now, it was tough to bring Crowley around to discussing Linda Spain.

'Jesus, Sidney will blow his top when he finds out about this,' I said sadly. 'He was nuts about that girl.'

'That's right, you got to feel sorry for Sid.' Champ shook his head at a fleeting memory. 'I like the boob. Maybe that's why I feel so bad about Linda.'

I leaned over him confidentially, struggling with obvious discomfort, so that he could see the effort it was taking to bend me his way in a burst of man-to-man camaraderie. 'Listen, Champ,' I said, 'on the level, do you think maybe it was Sidney who knocked her off last night?'

'Jesus!' he gasped, pulling away from me. 'You know something, I never thought of that angle.'

'I didn't either. Mostly because Sid's a pal of mine.'

'Sid doesn't throw his weight around.'

'Maybe he could if he got jealous, Champ.'

'Nuts,' said Champ with finality. 'He couldn't have done it, Art.'

'You sound positive. You think one of her other boyfriends knocked her off?'

'I don't know,' Champ speculated, taking his time to run through his memory for an answer. 'Listen, she didn't have any real steadies but Sid.'

'A queer dame, all right,' I said. 'Terrific, but a little bit missing upstairs, maybe. How long did you know her, Champ?'

'She's been in this place, let's see now, about six, seven months.' He took his time with the line, diddling with his glass and giving me a slow and significant roll of his eyes. Caution clouded his face, the sharpening look tightening his jaw as he stared at me curiously. He could be getting mad behind those eyes, but he would never explode because he had full control of his emotional machine. He had weathered the storm of suspicions before, and knew how to handle them. He put his glass down deliberately and leaned across the table, so close that I could smell the liquor on his breath. 'What are you trying to promote, Seton?' he asked quietly. 'You hinting that maybe I stepped in there last night and knocked her off?'

'Relax, Champ,' I said, lightening it up a little. 'You're clean in my book. I was just wondering about Sid, though. He might think the other way. Sid can get tough if he feels in the mood.'

'Tough?' The little jockey enjoyed the idea, chuckling over it, an obviously zany picture in his mind. 'He's as soft as a tub of butter inside.'

'Maybe yes, maybe no,' I said doubtfully. 'I've heard stories about him, Champ. Crazy stuff that's hard to believe.'

'What kind of stories?'

I took a minute out for a histrionic bout with my conscience, losing the first round and leaning closer to Champ. 'I hear he's made himself some pretty nasty enemies lately.'

'That's tough to swallow,' Champ said. 'Who could hate the fat boy?'

'I hear he's in with a bad bunch.'

'Are you serious?'

I shook my head thoughtfully. 'I'm not kidding, Champ. And from what I hear, neither are they. I met a character who told me Sid was tied up with the Monk Stang outfit.'

'Stang, the hood?' The jockey's face was a caricature of unfeigned astonishment. It was no act. He leaned away from me, elevated his eyebrows and stared at me. He gave me the full strength of his penetrating optics, searching me for a clue to my purpose. I played it straight and with a deadpan sorrow. I sold him my worry.

'That sounds fantastic,' Champ whispered. 'What the hell would he be doing with a bigtime mobster like Monk Stang?'

'Running errands for him, from what I hear.'

'Errands? What kind?'

But there was no point to any further pursuit of the subject. I had reached the end of the road with Champ Crowley. The clock had run out on our friendly exchange, and there were other fish for me to fry. I picked up my hat and set it on my head.

'Who knows what his job could be?' I asked myself. 'I was just as surprised as you when I heard about it, Champ. I just hope Sid's clean on this deal, or he might get himself into a bad fix.'

He escorted me to the door, clucking sympathetically. He had picked up much of my emotional upset, and seemed genuinely concerned about Sidney Wragge now.

'Poor Sid,' he said. 'It's going to be a big bang if he walks in and finds out about Linda. I didn't read anything about her in the morning paper. I wonder why?'

'The city dicks might be playing it smart,' I said. 'They figure they can trap the killer by keeping mum about it. I wish to hell I knew where to locate Sid. He might get himself into hot water if he comes waltzing up here. That's why I want to find him, Champ. I could save him a big headache.'

'Let me know how you make out,' Champ Crowley said at the door.

'You can count on me,' I said.

And when I walked away from him, he looked as though he believed me.

21

Spud's Midtown Snack Bar
6:00 P.M. — July 19th

I had covered a lot of ground since the sun burned my eyes awake on the rug in Linda Spain's living room. I was hungry enough to beat it inside the first beanery I found on my walk across the town. I sat alone in a small booth complete with gravy stains, tortured upholstery, and a good view of the street through the greasy window. I ordered some simple fare and sat there doodling sketches on the paper napkin before me. And the drawing came straight from my subconscious, hesitant at first, but strong and bold after a while, the first formative lines of the face of Sidney Wragge.

The waitress brought the soup and I abandoned my sketching for a try at deep and important thought. Nothing came to me. I stared through the murky window.

The range of my focus stretched the length and breadth of the glass, a giant screen for the activities on the street beyond. It was a stage, an oblong frame of animation, against which the traffic played and the pedestrian tide ebbed and flowed. I sipped my soup and gazed absently at the slice of New York life. A truck pulled up, discharged his cargo, and slid away at full steam. The noise of an organ grinder filtered through to me, and then he was passing, across the street, an aimless entertainer who turned his tune lazily as he walked. From somewhere on the river a tug hooted and tooted, the sound of the whistle ululating in the distances.

Then I saw the man in the green hat.

You look at a street and the people are all casual wanderers, appearing and disappearing beyond the frame of the window. They came and went, in one side and out the other. But having gone, they did not return. That was the gimmick. That was the clue to the man in the green hat.

I saw him first as part of a group,

across the street. He was walking slowly, reading a newspaper as he strolled. He faded out after that, to the right, lost to me. But he returned. And this time the newspaper was down. He swung it at his side, casually, slapping it against his shanks in the attitude of a man who walks with no purpose.

It was when he appeared the third time that he began to register. Now he sauntered close to the shop window across the street. He bent to examine the display in a tiny stationer's. He leaned against the window and flicked his eyes my way, an instant's pause, but enough to catch my eye. He was a bad actor, an obvious tail, a watcher who lacked the skill and sensibility of a seasoned operator. He crossed my range of vision once again, walking westward now. I lit a cigarette and sipped my coffee and watched the window for his return. He was doing things to my stomach. He was ruining my lunch, tightening my gut with a growing anger.

Who could be on my tail? I resisted the impulse to bound out of my chair and cross the street to him. Instead, I cased him carefully. He appeared for my examination, but this time I had my mental index wide open for filing him away. He was a middling-sized character, as faceless as a good tail should be. He was wearing a business suit, a double-breasted item of light brown. He had on a reddish tie, knotted tightly. But it was his greenish felt that stamped him and typed him and made him easy for me. And he wore glasses, heavy and of a darkish tortoiseshell. I paid my check and slid out into the street.

At the corner he was watching me from under the awning of a drugstore across the street. He made a big production out of reading his newspaper. I turned uptown, feeling my short hairs prickle in the instinctive reflex to pursuit. I played it deliberately dumb, giving him ample time to keep me in sight as I led him across town. It did my heart good to work him a little. He was not built for walking fast. He would puff and pant soon. The Rivington was across the park and he dropped back when I started under the trees, the proper procedure for following a man through the wide open spaces. When I emerged on the west side, he was far behind and mopping his fevered brow, a laughable figure far down the lane. I paused to sit and light a cigarette, allowing him to heave into view and freeze behind a tree.

Then I crossed the street and entered the lobby of the Rivington.

Toni greeted me with mixed emotions.

'Where have you been all this time?' she asked petulantly. She allowed me to kiss her, but there was nothing in it of her old heat and friendliness. 'I've been going nuts in this dump.'

'You haven't gone out?'

'Where in hell would I go?'

'I'm only asking,' I said. 'Because it could be bad business for you to leave this place.'

Her window faced the street, so that I had a bird's-eye view of the area from the edge of Central Park to the entrance below. The man in the green hat must have taken his lessons in investigation from a mail order school. He should have flunked out and gotten a refund. He was standing across the street, leaning into the shadows of an apartment house alley. He was as obvious as a hound dog over a bone. His hand was up to his overheated face, and he was mopping more sweat as he squinted up at the Rivington.

Toni joined me at the window.

'Did you come up here to look at the view?' she asked.

'You guessed it, Toni. Your window is hot.'

'What's hot about it? I've been staring out of it all day, and all I saw was yellow taxis.'

'Stare some more. Something new has been added.'

I lifted her phone and called the office. Izzy must have been waiting for my call.

I said, 'I've got news for you, Izzy. Things are looking up.'

'It's about time,' Izzy said. 'And maybe I've grabbed a small lead, too, Mike. The Sidney Wragge set-up begins to stink to high heaven. The layout at the Kimberly Building is out of this world, for instance. The dump leases their offices furnished.

All the paper stuff down there was meaningless. Wragge rented that place with the files loaded. The janitor reports him as just a casual visitor to his office. He was in there for maybe four months, but he only came to work about once a week, on the average. I tried to find out why, but I couldn't quite make it. The set-up just doesn't make any sense at all. The way I figure it, Wragge purely went there to sit and think.'

'Anybody on the floor know him?'

'A blank in that direction, too. And almost as blank at his apartment. His lease coincides with the rental of the office in the Kimberly Building, almost to the day. But nobody in the flat saw much of him except the janitor — seems as though Sidney made a bit of book for him.'

'It fits,' I said. 'He also took small wagers from a druggist up on the corner. Where are you headed next?'

'Back to his flat, Mike. I think I may dig something out of the tenants there. I like the apartment for background on him. I've got an idea — a small one, but it may be the opening we need.'

'What is it?'

'It won't make sense over the phone. But I want you to come down to his flat right away. Where are you? Can you come now?'

'Not quite,' I said. 'Somebody put a tail on me, Izzy.'

'When?' Izzy's voice cracked a bit with excitement. 'This, I like. Who sent him?'

I watched Toni react to my dialogue about the tail. She came alive at the window, her fingers twitching on the drapes as she stared down into the street. She began to gnaw on her lip, slid away from the window and crossed the room, pausing in her restlessness to lift an ashtray and carry it toward the john. She passed me on the way, close enough so that I could catch a fast squint at the ashtray. It was loaded.

The mind of an investigator operates through the stimulus of his vision. You open your eyes and the light hits against the wall of your intellect and the little things come into focus and become clear and challenging. All the minor items loom large and important in the filing cabinet brain of the man who searches. You stare around a room and let it speak to you in the silence. You listen for the voices that sometimes shout from a matchbox, or a cigarette butt, or the way two cushions are placed on a couch. And in this little pause, something in the room was banging away at my inner ear. Something important.

But Izzy was saying, 'What the hell happened to you, Mike? Fall into a sewer up there? I just asked you when you spotted the tail.'

Toni was back at my side again. I held her hand and eased her into a chair alongside me. She seemed to be quieter now, calmer.

I said, 'He showed himself when I left Champ Crowley's place. But he might have been on me longer. He might have been on me last night, for all I know.'

'Grab him and find out,' Izzy almost commanded. 'He may be a key to something we need. Or do you want me to come up and do it while you play games with the doll?'

'Not on your life. This character is for me.'

'Good boy. Who do you think sent him out, Mike?'

'He leaves me cold.'

'He could be one of Leach's boys,' Izzy suggested.

'Not this boob. I don't know Leach's staff, but if he trained his boys to move the way this jerk operates, Leach needs help with his squad. This one is much too square for a city dick. The guy's obvious — a private op, for my dough.'

'Get him!' said Izzy. 'And when you find out who sent him, meet me at Wragge's flat.'

'Give me an hour,' I said. 'I'll be there.'

22

'Forget about him, Toni,' I said.

'Is that supposed to make me develop amnesia?' she asked.

'I'll get rid of him soon — and permanently. You've got nothing to worry about, I tell you.'

But she was hell-bent for worry in a big way, a dramatic way, complete with a flurry of nervous energy that sent her out of control. She was hypnotized by the window. She stood there, making sorry faces at the landscape beyond. She was petulant, and capable of anger and hard words in a crisis like this. It did something to her face I hadn't noticed before, promoting her beauty in a strange way, so that I felt like playing with her, suddenly, to take her mind off the street.

'Pull the shade down if he worries you,' I said.

'It won't help.'

'Maybe I can help?'

She leaned into me and buried her head in my chest. 'I'm all mixed up, Mike.'

'Break it down for me and I'll rub it out, Toni.'

'It's this room, I guess. It gripes me. It keeps reminding me of what might happen if this thing ever breaks into print — about me, I mean.'

'Show business?'

'That's it. It'd ruin me.'

'You won't find it in the papers.'

'I won't?' She came alive now, sighing with relief. 'You kept it out?'

'Not quite. But the police don't want it released yet.'

'Isn't that unusual?'

'They're playing it smart,' I said. 'Because the fat man's girlfriend was murdered last night.'

Toni shivered and sank into the easy chair. 'That's awful, Mike. What does it mean? What does the whole stinking mess mean? Who was the girl?'

'A burlesque doll — name of Linda Spain. She was knifed.'

'Horrible. The poor girl. Who would do it?'

'They thought I did it.'

'You?'

'I was there, Toni.'

Now she was angry and impatient again. 'The fools! Why should they suspect you? Can't they see that you were dragged in by the heels? It doesn't make sense, Mike.' And she stared at me incredulously, the light of sympathy warming her big eyes. 'How in hell can you take it? How can you keep your head?'

'Part of my business. I've been through it before.'

'You know what you're going to do next?'

'I know what I'm going to try.'

'You're wonderful, Mike.'

'Not wonderful — desperate. I've got to go out and get me some more research.' I strolled back to the window, flipped the shade, and looked down into the street. He was there. 'The little man bothers me.'

'Why should he be following you?'

'I'm going to find out.'

'But how?'

'By simply asking him a question or two.'

'Please,' she pleaded, holding me at the door. 'You sure you know what you're doing, Mike? He could be dangerous. You might get hit again.'

'There's only one way to finger a tail,' I said, working myself loose from her demanding hands. 'What I said before about you still goes. Stay right where you are.'

'But how long?'

'Until I come back. I've got to meet Izzy down at the fat boy's flat. Izzy sounds as though he's got something. But it shouldn't take me long. Stay put.'

'I'm going nuts up here alone.'

'Do as you're told, Toni.'

I went down into the lobby and crossed before the desk so that I could get an angle shot of the street from one side of the hall. He was still out there, busying himself with a cigarette and shifting his weight from one leg to the other. He would be good and tired now. I walked back through the hall to the door with the red light over it. I stepped downstairs into the basement, a catacomb of shadows, loaded with the debris usually found in hotel cellars. Beyond the crates and boxed sections for storage, on the other side of the square stone room, a pale blue light burned above a door. It was the way out. I doubled back through the alley and climbed a fence to get through to the next building, on the side that faced Central Park West. Here another narrow alley led me to the pavement facing the park.

Across the street, I scuttled quickly along the stone wall and made my way back a half-block, so that I could re-cross again beyond his focus, shielded from him by the building against which he leaned. It was another small hotel, and here the service entrance was easy to enter. It led me back into a small, square yard. On the other side, the street was separated from this area by a heavy metal fence. The ramp leading up to his fence brought me within a few feet of the man in the green hat. I cat-walked up to him. The street was empty when I came up behind him, fast enough to make my approach dramatic and surprising. He was an easy grab.

I jerked him hard, a back hold that caught him and riveted him because he was unprepared for my assault, stumbling against me and almost throwing me off-balance on the incline. He struggled desperately when he knew the score, which was a split second after I had him. He was equipped for breaking judo grips, more wiry than I expected. It did my heart good to level him with a strong right to his navel as soon as he turned my way. He groaned and gurgled his pain. He doubled up and rolled quietly down the incline to the basement steps.

I dragged him into the shadows and sat all over him, slapping him until his face was redder than the Communist banner. His hat fell off, and he was a middle-aged and balding character. He had a flabby face, and eyes that were as strong as noodle soup. If I continued to massage him, he might collapse completely. He had used the dying remnants of a once-athletic frame in the one desperate flurry up on the ramp. He was as limp and life-less as Monday's wash now. I clutched his suit, high on the lapels. I jerked his head up.

'Who sent you out?' I asked.

'Drop dead,' he answered.

'You want to play some more?' I slapped his head back against the concrete wall behind him, a flat crack that brought his tongue out of his mouth. 'Who sent you?'

'You heard me before.'

'I'm losing my patience.'

'Go lose it somewhere else,' he said. 'You bother me.'

So I bothered him some more. He asked for it. He asked for the full flood of my pent-up impatience, the frustration and anger that had been building in me for moments like this. He was shorter and weaker than I, but no qualm of sympathy rose up to alter my purpose. Anger bit deep inside me and I struck out at him again, this time with my fist, straight for his jaw.

He was out, and I dragged him down the steps and into the basement. I frisked him quickly and found an automatic under his jacket. There was a sink down there, and I heaved a bucket of water at him, stunning him to wakefulness again. I stood there over him and waited for his eyes to stop rolling. And then I showed him the gun.

A gun can be magic. A gun can be *open sesame* for the stubborn mouth of a character like the man on the floor beneath me. He popped his eyes at the gun. He squirmed away from it, holding up his hands and going whole hog on the terror routine. He pushed his body against the wall as though he might find a hole there and disappear forever from the muzzle before him.

'Who sent you out?' I asked again.

'Rico Bruck,' he said.

'Why?'

'Rico didn't tell me.'

'You're one of his boys?'

He bobbled his head at me, out of breath and weak with fear. 'Masters,' he gasped. 'George Masters is my name. Private investigator.'

'Prove it.'

He proved it. His hand snaked into his

jacket pocket and came out with a wallet, through which he fumbled for a card of identification. What I saw on the card almost made me laugh out loud. The poor slob was a downtown dick, a private op. He watched me nervously, mopping the blood from his cracked lip.

'As one private eye to another, Masters, you stink.'

'You?' he asked wearily. 'Rico didn't tell me you were in the business.'

'What did Rico tell you?'

'Only to tail you.'

'When did you begin?'

'Yesterday,' he said.

'You didn't get much, did you?' I asked. 'I could have told Rico just where I was headed. All he had to do was ask me. But this pitch sort of changes things now.'

'Rico's all right. Don't blame Rico, pal.'

'Go back and tell him I love him dearly.'

'My rod, chum,' he said as I started away.

'I may need this gun.'

I stashed it away and went out through the alley, up the incline to the street. I ran to the corner and grabbed a cab there.

23

Sweat! The incident with the man named Masters had tightened me and heated me and forced my mind into the narrow groove that always comes at the end of a chase. I sat back in the cab and listened to the noises of the night as we sped through the downtown lanes of traffic that would carry me to Sidney Wragge's apartment. The hiss and hum of the tires should have wooed me into a relaxed mood, but my brain was singing with the thousand and one words I would soon exchange with Izzy. I added up my stockpile of odds and ends, and found the total interesting. There were areas of emptiness and speculation, but I knew that Izzy and I would fill the gaps, just as soon as we sat in a quiet corner and laid out the strange pattern of evidence that began with the murder of the fat man. I burned with the yen to tell Izzy about Masters. If Rico had hired him to tail me, it really meant that we could cross Bruck off our list of suspects. Obviously the little Chicago gambler couldn't have killed Wragge if he suspected me of having the Folsom pendant. Whoever murdered Wragge had that pendant!

I was running when I left the cab, through the dingy hall of Wragge's apartment, and down the corridor to his rooms.

'I've got something, Izzy!' I said, bursting in.

A dull lamp lit only one corner of the fat man's room. I stepped back in a reflex of horror as I saw what lay under the small table near the window. Izzy Rosen was on the floor. He was seated in a grotesque pose against the wall, his head down in the attitude of a tired drinker at an all-night brawl. But what had leveled Izzy was much stronger than a party cocktail. Somebody had hit him. Somebody had opened his head with a vicious blow behind the right ear, a bloody welt that made my stomach toss.

I ran into the john, got a glass of water and held it to his lips. He was too far gone for helping himself. And the sight of him on the floor tore at my heart and made me mutter profanities at the unknown bastard who had slugged him.

'Mike — '

He barely said the word, letting it bubble from his tired, bumbling lips, and tried to open his eyes for me.

'Who slugged you, Izzy?'

His head rolled weakly to one side and went limp and lifeless. He was out cold now, and it would do no good to try and talk with him. I grabbed the phone and called for an ambulance, caught up in the hopelessness of watching my best friend fall away from me. I hung up and beat my fists and listened to the sound of my anger, the desperate pounding in my head. The words I had for Izzy rose up in me, so that I began to whisper them to the four walls. Whoever mauled him must have thought that we were coming down to the wire on the Sidney Wragge case. Why? What drove the zany sneak to

Wragge's apartment? And who was he?

The wail of the ambulance tore me out of my reverie. I rode it back to the hospital, where I watched them cart Izzy away, and sat in the waiting room for a long time. The events of the past two days skittered through my mind; I closed my eyes against them and tried for some order, some plan. But the worry about my partner rose up to cancel out all intelligent thought. Anger boiled in me, enough to bring me to my feet and set me to pacing the quiet room.

And then a nurse came out and said, 'No use waiting any longer. He's in a coma. We don't know when he'll come out of it.'

'How bad is it?'

'Concussion.'

'I want to see the doctor.'

'I'm sorry, but you can't.' She was using her quiet and professional softness, trying to calm me.

'It's important.'

'It's impossible.'

'The hell it is,' I said. 'It's important for me to know when he comes out of it.

He'll be saying things I want to hear. I figure he'll be telling me who slugged him, and that means a lot to me, sister.'

'I know how you feel, but there isn't any way to get you inside to see the doctor now.' She eyed me with a show of friendliness. 'But maybe I can help you. I'll stay with him.'

She began to come into focus for me. Sometimes the heat of anxiety can dull the visual machinery. A few minutes ago she was only a blob of white femininity, the symbol of a nurse, out of perspective for me because my brain wasn't interested in any of the intimate details of her figure. She had existed as a formless thing, in the same way that the pictures on the wall were only dull squares of nothing against a colorless background. But now her voice came through to me and the undertones were husky and exciting. And, after her voice, I was beginning to notice her face: the smooth, round oval of a beautiful peasant, blue-eyed and challenging and provocative.

'Well, that's nice of you, Miss — ?'

'Prionee.'

'Is that what your friends call you?'

'You can call me Magda.' She blushed prettily and smoothed her uniform. 'And don't worry about your friend. I'll take care of him.'

'I'm not worried anymore, Magda.'

But I was worried sick, and the worry built in me to become a tight knot of blossoming disquiet, until I found myself in a convenient bar, downing my third hooker of Scotch and making sour faces at the glass. There was a newspaper under my eyes, but the print seemed blurred and fogged as I thumbed through it, skimming the pages willy-nilly. Was my brain seeking some mention of the Sidney Wragge case? Were my eyes flitting purposely over the headlines? I found myself reading the Broadway gossip column of an elf named Arch Minton, a news maggot who had a variety of scouts in every hot spot in town. And Arch was reporting a strange piece of news. Arch said: 'A little bird tells me that Monk Stang and two of his boys are spending the weekend in a cool room downtown. Rent free, yet!'

So the police had jailed Stang and his henchmen! I had been toying with the idea of paying Monk Stang a visit, to talk again of his reasons for visiting New York, to ask him cute questions about Frenchy Armetto and Max. Now I could cross those three off my mental inventory. Now I could begin to fight my way back through the recent past, working to organize the card index file of memory, to prime myself for the next move in the zany hunt for Sidney Wragge's killer. The next move? Where was it?

My impatience worked against any intelligent thought. I was too upset about Izzy to concentrate with any planned purpose. I sat there sucking hard at my cigarette, watching the elbow-benders at the bar and listening to the jukebox grind out the monotonous rhythm of a current polka. On my right, a grizzled bartender leaned confidentially toward a man with a pink, bald head. A fan buzzed from somewhere deep in the dirty shadows. Beyond the misted window, the lights of the street were fogged and dim, the noises out there blurred and muted. A taxi horn brayed at a traffic light. Someone laughed from far away.

Then the door opened and a couple walked in, the girl giddy and high, the boy alive with quiet purpose, his eyes nibbling at her as they approached the bar and sat down. She pulled coyly at the loose strands of blonde hair that fell over her shoulder. She was a chorine, well-made-up and round and soft in the figure. She primped in the mirror behind the bar. The gesture caught and held me. It was a familiar movement, a quick flick of the fingers that stimulated me because it reminded me of someone out of the recent past. She was squirming on the stool now, moving her hips in a delectable motion. Her head turned my way and I saw then that it couldn't be her face that challenged me. She was not pretty. But something about the color of her hair was setting off a chain reaction in my mind. A blonde! The silken sheen forced me off on a one-way tour in my mental hayride. She was backing me into a recent corner, forcing my brain into those hectic moments with Toni Kaye.

Toni! The thought of her was enough to move me. Off my chair and out through the bar and into the street.

Because suddenly a fresh wave of anger had made my spine crawl with purpose. I knew where I was going now.

I skipped off the curbing and began to yell for a cab.

24

The Rivington Hotel
9:53 P.M. — July 19th

The Rivington was a gray and ghostly shape in the rain, as dim and misted as an Impressionist painting, but twice as inspirational for me. I paid off the cabby and stood across the street from the ancient canopy, letting my eyes play games with the stone facade while my brain groped and fiddled for the right approach to Toni Kaye. She was awake. Her window was an oblong of yellow light up there. In moments like this, a private eye plays games with his ego. The heat of the chase boiled up in me. There were a few dozen ways for handling Toni, but I wanted the one perfect approach. I wanted the way that would make her talk, and the memory of her sharp mind slowed me down and forced me into plans of strategy, like a corn-fed hero in a television mystery.

Toni was clever. Toni was intelligent. I had figured her all wrong, from the moment I met her on the pebbled drive of Rico Bruck's Chicago den. How long ago? I almost laughed out loud when I backed into the past and realized that so much had happened in less than a week.

And then I thought of Izzy Rosen.

And I flipped my cigarette away and ran across to the Rivington.

Toni let me in with a tired yawn. She had a two-bit romance in her hand, and rubbed her eyes to prove that she had been reading it. It might have been true, because the couch was arranged for the chore. She had dragged the small end table up to the edge of the sofa, and the little lamp still burned, and the pillows still showed the imprint of her body. No other light was alive in the room, and the pat stage set irritated me. I reached for the wall switch.

Toni blinked and said, 'Must you?'

I took off my jacket and threw it on a chair. 'I don't like being in the dark, Toni.'

'And what does that mean?'

'Just that I like you in the clear, so that

211

I can eat you with my eyes.'

'Flatterer.' She smiled and started toward me from the window, more graceful in slippers than she was in high heels. She had on a lounging outfit that seemed fresh and new, a silken ensemble that did little to hide her provocative figure. She stretched as she came, and her gesture was slow and contrived, like a young actress working at being the *femme fatale*. Or was my imagination playing tag with me? Were her eyes a bit too bright after a session with a book? And her make-up? Was it fresh and brilliant suddenly? I watched her move my way, her hips swaying gently. And then she was sitting alongside me on the couch, and the air around me was alive with her personal perfume.

And she was saying, 'You look all in, Mike. Tired?'

'Sick and tired.'

'Nothing new?'

'You mean with Izzy?' I shook my head wearily. 'Sometimes even Izzy goes off on a false lead. He was all wrong about the last one.'

'That's a shame,' she said quietly She

got up and showed me that my news upset her. 'I suppose that means I'll be holed up in this rat nest forever?'

I didn't answer. My eyes had begun their tour of the room. There were three ashtrays, all of them glass, of the common variety found in cheap hotels. The one at my elbows had two butts, each of them tipped with crimson.

'Is it such a bad place?' I asked.

'Bad? It's horrible. The monotony is killing me.'

'I'll rent you a television set.'

'No, thanks. That would really give me headaches.'

The second ashtray, on the coffee table near the easy chair, was empty. The third one was near the wall, on another table. I got up and went to Toni, turned her around and let her feel my arms. She was tight and stiff, promoting her restlessness by going metallic for me.

'You'll only have to take it for a little while longer,' I said.

'How long?'

'A day — two days.'

'Jesus, I don't think I can take it.'

Her eyes telegraphed the worry and confusion that was supposed to be gnawing at her. Then I pulled her tight to me and looked down over her shoulder. On the table, the third ashtray was empty. In the split second of my discovery, laughter bubbled in me. I felt like the cornball dick in a half-hour detective opera, burning his eyes out for the usual clues, the little signs, the impossible, ridiculous, expected gimmicks of story-book investigation. But the laughter simmered down and died in my gut. I saw what I hoped for. There were several lumpy shreds of brown and stringy tobacco on the slick surface of the table.

I fought down the dirty names that rose in my throat. There would be time for hot words a little later in our dramatic joust. Right now I struggled to keep it crisp and enjoyable, in the way that a director might relish watching the try-outs for a bit part in a Broadway play. It tickled me to see that she was steering me back to the couch, and sitting close to me again, and leaning into me to show me how her body trembled.

On the floor, near the white pompom of her slipper, there were more tobacco curlings.

'Don't let it throw you,' I told her, letting her bury her scented head on my shoulder and then kissing her when she brought her head up. 'This place isn't so bad. Matter of fact, I think it's quite comfortable.'

'That isn't it, Mike,' she whispered tragically. 'The whole crazy set-up scares me.'

'You're still worried about Bruck?'

'You know I am.'

'Suppose I told you to forget about him?'

Her body went cold again under my hand. Or was it only the reflex stiffening of her figure as she pulled herself up and away from me? She was staring at me, her bright eyes a mixture of confusion and incredulity. Her play-acting might have been genuine yesterday, but right now it was as phony as an eight-year-old wearing falsies.

'Are you serious?' she asked.

'Forget about Rico Bruck.'

'But how can you say that, Mike?'

'I can say it because I know he doesn't give a damn about you anymore. Rico and I had a little talk.'

What flickered in her bright eyes now? In the split second it took to drop the few words, a spark of caution seemed to flame. Or was it fear? But it faded fast, to be replaced by her tender smile, complete with the full view of her little white teeth, a symbol of girlish relief. Her husky laughter followed, and then she was leaning over me again and telling me her joy with her body and her mouth. I let her go the full course. She was stalling for time. She was laying into me, using her phony passion to prepare herself for the next move in my little game. My imaginative double-talk goosed me into strange and subtle paths of thought. She would be a strange and misfit bedmate for little Rico. She would be yearning for greater conquests, quietly watching the crowds at the Card Club, making her pitch for the more important types, because Toni Kaye yearned for show business passion, complete with all the side dishes.

'Then Rico knows all about us?' she asked.

'He knows — and he doesn't give a damn,' I lied. 'All Rico wants is a small cluster of diamonds, Toni. Rico has a one-track mind, or didn't you know?'

'I know him well.' She shivered. 'But I never heard him mention diamonds.'

'Not even the Folsom pendant?'

'What's the Folsom pendant?'

'Don't you read the papers?' I asked.

'I must have missed that story.'

'Not if you read the headlines.'

She had made her first mistake, but her shrewd and conniving brain picked it up. And fast. She assumed a thoughtful and serious air, and snapped her elegant fingers, and suddenly remembered all about the Folsom pendant.

'The big robbery in Chicago. Of course,' she said.

'Now you're back on the beam again. You must have heard some gossip about it in the Card Club.'

'Rico never mentioned it to me.'

'And how about Gilligan?'

'Gilligan? I hardly know him.'

I got off the couch and lit a cigarette and walked to the corner of the room where the bottles were. I filled a glass, and let her watch me and wonder about me. She was uncomfortable in the gap of silence, just the way I wanted her to be. When the chips are down, and the quarry is cornered and trembling, dead air can solve many problems. It was an old police trick I had learned long time ago. You drop the bait. You sit and wait. You are in the position of a professional psychologist who knows the mechanics of emotion. I had needled her skillfully, pricking the nerve ends of her secret self. It was time for the knife now.

'You know him,' I said.

'Well, of course I know him, Mike. But only casually.'

'You know him well.'

'You're crazy,' she said, still trying for fresh laughter. But the impact of my deadpan stare was bringing her off the couch. She bounced to her feet with a nervous leap. 'What are you trying to say?'

'I'm not trying. I'm saying it.'

'That I know Gilligan well?'

'Intimately.'

'But you're all wrong, Mike.'

'You're lying,' I said flatly, moving closer to her. 'You and Gilligan are close enough for playing games.' She stepped back from me, the upset shining in her big eyes, riveted on me with the fascinated stare of a rabbit watching a cobra. And when I grabbed her, she went stiff and tight. 'Bedroom games,' I added.

'That's fantastic,' Toni said, whipping herself the other way, out of my arms and back toward the couch. Now the dramatics were pitched high and tense, and her impatience with me came through with exaggerated gestures. I had grabbed her hard, and she worked to rub the hurt away, massaging her arms where my fingers had bit into them. Her mouth curled in a disdainful smirk, and her face clouded with intemperate evil. 'If you want to be jealous, pick somebody logical, Mike. Pick somebody I really like. But not Gilligan.'

'I'll stick with Gilligan.'

'But why? I can't understand what's

happened to you.' Now her voice softened and quivered and she moved again. I was in the easy chair near the window, and she drifted my way and showed me her damp eyes. She sat on the arm, and when she put a hand on mine, her fingers were as cold as a plucked chicken. She breathed hard. But her histrionics were all stale and old now. 'What's come over you, Mike?'

'Gilligan,' I said, and grabbed her wandering hands. 'Gilligan was here, wasn't he?'

'Now I know you're out of your head.'

'I'll play it again. Gilligan was here.'

'You're hurting my hands.'

I pulled her down closer to me, so that her face became a mask, a caricature of frightened womanhood. And when I could count the eyelashes around her beautiful eyes, I said it again. 'Gilligan was here. Admit it.'

'It isn't true, Mike.'

So I slapped her high on the right cheek. The flat crack of my hand sent her falling back into the chair, and her face went dead and cold under the power of the blow. Something glowed deep under her mascaraed eyes, an animal violence that died quickly, to be replaced by tears.

She ran into the bedroom and slammed the door behind her. So I followed her inside. She was on the bed, her head buried in the pillow. I sat alongside her and jerked her around so that her tear-stained face looked up at me. The dewy sorrow had blackened her cheeks with mascara and there were two burning spots high on her jaws. The room was lit only by the subdued radiance from outside, the intermittent blinking of an electric sign on the hotel across the street.

'Please, Mike,' she murmured. 'You hurt me.'

'Gilligan was here,' I said. 'Admit it.'

I grabbed out at her and pulled her upright. I swung her around and suddenly she was all animal. She clawed for my face and her nails knifed my neck and I heard her mutter a foul and evil name. She bounced off the bed and slid to the right and fell to the floor where her luggage lay. Her hands were groping for something down there, but she didn't have the time. She might have been reaching for an automatic. She might have been diving for a hidden knife. She found nothing but the hard edge of my hand as I tugged her away and hit her again.

It was enough to wilt her. She was all limp and loose when I lifted her to the bed. She was out. Cold.

I doused her with a glass of water and stood back, watching her eyelids flicker and move back into consciousness. She squirmed slowly on the sheet, and the muscles around her mouth worked hard to bring her face under control.

'You big bastard,' she said.

I went to her luggage, flipped it open, and pulled out a small and dainty revolver, buried under her silken slips. She came awake when I showed it to her, when I put the muzzle close to her cheek and let it linger there. She backed deep into the pillow, and stiffened as the gun followed her.

'Now, about Gilligan,' I said. 'He was here. I know he was here because I found traces of him, don't you see? He left some of his stinking collegiate tobacco around. He tapped his pipe in the wrong places, a habit he's had since his schoolboy days. He was up here today, because you damn near broke your neck getting his tobacco shreds out of the room when I called Izzy Rosen, remember? You became the neat and fussy type all of a sudden, and that was what started me thinking about Gilligan.'

'Very clever.'

'I get better as I go on,' I said. I dropped the gun so that the cold steel rested above her heart. 'You called Gilligan after I left to meet Izzy, didn't you?'

'You're out of your mind.'

'Am I? Want me to check with the switchboard downstairs?'

Something died in her eyes. I didn't push her anymore. I stood over her and let her simmer down. She was cracking completely, trembling now, kneading her hands and shaking her head hopelessly. This was no act. Her little game was over, and she knew it. She tugged her blouse around her and continued to stare at the corner of the rug, sobbing real sobs now.

'I called Gilligan,' she whispered.

'Why?'

'I was working for him, Mike. All the way from Chicago. He wanted me to stay with you, to throw a pitch for you the minute you walked into the Card Club. He paid me a lot of money for the job.'

'What else?'

'That's all I know.'

'How many times did you see him since we arrived in New York?'

'Only twice.'

'Where?'

'At the Brentworth, yesterday — when you were tailing the fat man.'

'He came to our room?'

She broke it down for me, all the way. Gilligan had paid her a visit to give her instructions, to warn her that she must stay close to me and keep him informed. But Toni knew nothing of his purpose. I barraged her with questions. How about Bruck? Was Bruck in the deal, too? Was Bruck paying off for Toni to follow me? No, she had her orders only from Gilligan. How much was Gilligan paying?

Two grand, plus a promise to get her started in show business.

'And what did Gilligan want this morning?' I asked.

'More information. He questioned me about the Linda Spain murder. He wanted to know whether you had told me anything about it, anything at all.'

'He must have been disappointed.'

'He didn't stay long.' Toni squirmed on the bed, uncomfortable now, as though the memories of her intimacy with Gilligan were eating away at her mind. She leveled her eyes at me, and something of her original softness crept back into her gaze, the warmth and excitement she had used on me back in the Card Club. But the old charm was gone for me, and she knew it. She sat there, chewing her lip and saying nothing.

'Get dressed,' I said.

'Must I, Mike?'

She got up, saying nothing, the hopelessness filling her face. She took off her blouse and stood there for a tick of time: a last, desperate try. But how could she know that I was thinking of Izzy

Rosen at that moment? How could she know that my stomach knotted when I thought of him on the floor in Wragge's apartment, the blood spilling out of him? How could she guess that the sight of her pink and tender skin only built great waves of hate in me?

I repeated, 'Get dressed. You and I are going out together.'

25

Toni was a nuisance, but an important one, and I could think of no safe nest where I might hide her away until needed. So she stepped at my side, a sulky siren, saying nothing, doing nothing but chain smoke and glare at me whenever my face was turned her way. I cautioned her against making a break in any direction. I warned her that I'd take her down to the station and leave her with Leach's boys, and she believed me all the way.

She said nothing on the way over to Wragge's flat in the taxi. Did she know the place? When the cab rolled up to the curbing, she looked out at the apartment with restrained petulance.

'May I ask what we're doing here?' she said, at the door.

'You may not,' I told her. 'Step inside — and keep your dainty little trap shut.'

Once inside, I forgot about Toni.

It was the room that gnawed at my weary brain. I stood flat-footed in the center of the rug. I gawked at the scattered debris on the floor. What had Izzy seen here? What had he found to excite him? The wall bed was down, and the sheets and pillowcases rumpled and wrinkled the way I had last seen them. The silence beat at my ears, echoing the rhythm of my anxiety, the pulse beat of my impatience to get on with the search.

'What are you looking for?' Toni asked.

'The lost chord.'

'Very funny. I thought I could help you.'

'The only way you'll help me is by clamming up.'

She bit her lip and remained silent. It would have been good if she were a helpmate. The game of hunt-and-squint is always easier with a companion. But what could I tell her to help me find, even if she could be used? What was I looking for?

I lit a cigarette, sat on the edge of the bed, and let the room sing to me, every small part of it, beginning at the door and advancing through the tiny corridor. I set myself on the short end of a mental microscope and took my mind on a ferret's search of every inch of the place. I built the huge figure of Sidney Wragge out of my meandering memory. I strained and struggled to make him a whole man again, entering his own apartment, coming through the door and across this rug. I sat him in the chair at the window and made him walk through all the casual movements of his life in this nest. Habit would take him to certain corners. Habit might help me mark him, label him, track down the fragile thread of his background. I followed him down the paths I had created for him, and the activity warmed me so that I began to sweat, and the walls crawled close to me and tore at my natural claustrophobia. The sweat dripped as I clung to the idiotic game that brought me to my knees on the rug, examining it for God-knew-what that Izzy might have seen.

Crazy? I must have looked out-and-out stupid to Toni. She got out of her chair and started away.

'Back where you were,' I told her, not looking up above her gams.

'I was only going to get you some water, Mike.'

'Back,' I said. 'I'll get my own drink.'

'Mind if I have one?'

I let her follow me into the tiny kitchenette, stumbling about among the scattered utensils on the gray linoleum. It came to me that I had neglected the kitchen altogether. Had Wragge hidden the pendant here? He might have borrowed a stunt from the farmer's wife and cached the gems in a sugar bowl or a cookie jar. He might have gone modern and hidden the stones in the ice tray, the way the fiction dicks do it on television. But every container capable of holding anything larger than salt and pepper lay open on the floor.

The water was sickeningly warm, and Toni reached for the trays of cubes in the refrigerator. She made a face at the display of food on the shelves. I pulled her away from the box and stood there, my mind on fire with a sudden thought. Did Izzy see what I was looking at? Had he been just as shocked?

Sidney Wragge's larder was a challenge. On the lower shelf sat a large bowl, and I lifted it out and stared into it.

'Phew!' said Toni.

'What is it?'

'Bacon fat, I think. But corroded.'

'You mean old?'

'Ancient.'

The bowl was of the family variety, usually used for serving up vegetables. How long had Sidney Wragge saved this grease? My mind stalled and balked at the picture of the fat man over a stove, cooking in this ancient lard, meticulously saving his bacon drippings for the next day's repast. He wasn't the type. He would be more at home in the Gourmet Society, fiddling with canapés and truffles, mixing intricate sauces and rubbing garlic tenderly in wooden salad bowls.

And the rest of the food in his box was just as ridiculous. Another smaller dish held the leavings of three boiled potatoes, a pale and greenish color. There were several bottles of cheap soda pop up high near the ice; a variety of liquid refreshment favored by small boys only, a sickly-sweet drink called Lemona. Had Sidney Wragge quenched his thirst with such drainage as this? Was he the type to munch stale and drab potato leavings?

'Foo!' said Toni, easing out a worn veal cutlet, stale and old and half gnawed away. 'This fat man sure was a slob when it came to leftovers.'

She was right, of course. Any schoolboy would have come to the same conclusion here. I began to check it through my mental adding machine. The mind of a detective is a strange and delicate instrument, a sieve through which the flotsam and jetsam of assorted information and inspiration must be forever strained and filtered and filed away for future reference. Once before, long ago, I had gained a head start on a weird assignment by correctly appraising a woman's closet. The intimate corners of a nest always reveal character. You look at a lampshade and guess at the buyer's taste. You sniff a perfume, and your mind clicks into a reflex judgment of the woman who wears the smell.

And this icebox? What was it telling me? How could this mess of garbage and goo belong to such a man as Sidney Wragge? No man on earth could develop such a contradicting series of personal tabs. Was he schizophrenic? Was he a Jekyll and Hyde? The idea sang with a high, sharp note in my tired head. I found myself back once again in Linda Spain's little love nest, staring in amusement at the bad painting Wragge had bought her. I found myself weighing the incense burner and placing it on the growing list of incongruities. And finally, when I began to add it all up, Linda Spain herself became the crowning idiocy in Wragge's roster of personal belongings. And something suddenly clicked and fell into place as I slammed the refrigerator door shut and decided to get out of there.

But at that moment the lights went out. Somebody came in. There was a stirring in the tiny corridor beyond the living room and I heard Toni suck in a deep sigh of astonishment.

'Elmo!' she said.

Then I saw him. I clawed back at the refrigerator handle in a desperate gesture that might bring me light. The door swung open and gave me a square of illumination, but not enough to define him clearly. The room heaved for me. The movement of Elmo exploded in my face. There was a moment when I saw the skulking shape moving in on me, and after that he was on me and all over me, forcing me back so that the door banged shut again and we were rolling and bouncing on the assorted pots and pans.

He was big. In the first flickering moment of his assault he hit me with his full weight, a ton of fat and muscle, an elephantine bulk who knew how to use his great and ponderous frame. He crashed against me and the breath sailed out of me, leaving me gasping and reaching feebly for the automatic I had taken from Masters. But there would be no time for firearms. He brought down his huge hands, blowing his hot and dirty breath into me, grunting and grumbling as he tried for my face. A filthy word escaped his lips and filtered through the heat of our struggle, and the word made me manic.

I said his name and the sound of it worked to unleash the needed fire in me, reminding me of my last fracas with him, so that I tried for his midriff, kicking up at him in the French style of fighting. I kneed him finally, a lusty blow that found the weak portion of his groin. I heard him grunt, and then he went soft above me and I knew that it was time for the other knee.

In the same place.

Elmo sucked air and clawed at his gut as I found a convenient skillet and beat his head with it. I heard him gasp and he slid away, and for a time I lost sight of his hands. But he showed them to me a moment later. And he had a gun in one of them. He brought it down against my head, a flat and leveling blow; a quick and metallic crash that sent me spinning out of the immediate gloom into a deeper and blacker pit. I was out again.

And paralyzed.

26

The hole I fell into was deep and dark, and at the bottom of it there was water, because I splashed into it, over my head and gurgling in my private bubble bath. Down where I was, only the sound of my own internal twitching bothered me, until a pixie with a big mop began to slap my face. And I started to yell at the pixie, but no sounds came from my blubbering lips. The persistent pixie continued to massage me with the mop, and I clawed out at it but didn't quite make contact with the elusive figure.

Until I woke up and saw that the pixie was Toni and the mop was a dishrag and the dishrag was slapping against my face. I was back in Wragge's kitchen. Beyond Toni, the dim, ponderous shape of Elmo loomed over me.

'Get the bastard up!' he said.

'Give him a chance to come around,' Toni said.

He grunted, and allowed her to slap me alive. After a while it began to sting, but I played it dull and dismal, wanting time for thought, quieting the fresh rash of anger that clawed at me when I opened my eyes a crack and saw Toni's elegant gams.

'Get up, sucker,' she said.

Elmo stepped forward and prodded my behind with the edge of his shoe. I got up slowly. He had his gun in my ribs and was pushing me toward the door. Toni led the way out to the street and into a big Caddy, as black as my immediate future. She opened the door to the rear seat, and Elmo came around and shoved me inside. Then he brought down his ape's hand again and clipped me with the gun. Just like that.

There was a space of nothingness, and this time no damp and bubbling pool came up to slap my face. I was adrift in a concrete mixer, a coffee grinder, a Mixmaster, and a pneumatic drill sent off sparks and made my head sing with angry pain. The last sound I heard was the hoarse bellow of a humorous bull, a grating laugh from Elmo. Beyond that, Toni was saying something, but it was soon lost to me in the personal miasma that hemmed me in. I was on the floor and eating a small segment of the rug. I was spitting dust and rolling over for air. From somewhere far in the next country, a fillip of sound crawled through to my brain and I knew that I was coming through the mist. How long had it taken? Minutes? Hours?

'You don't have to hit him again,' Toni was saying.

'I hate the bastard,' Elmo laughed. 'When we get there, I'm gonna pull his eyes out.'

'Where are you taking him?'

'Out on the Island.'

Was her foot snaking alongside my shoulder? I froze and tried to see her without breathing, without moving my body.

'Why the Island?' Toni asked.

'I know a good place. Water.'

'Why in the water?'

'The boss wants it should look like suicide. That makes it nice for me.'

'What's the name of the place?'

'A dump called Freeport.'

What was happening to her foot? The shoe came slowly back to skim my thigh and then it was snaking up again, rubbing me. Talking to me? The car was on a smooth highway now, and there were no traffic lights to hold Elmo to a decent pace. I was on my way to hell in a hack, on a one-way trip to cool water, but too much of it. It was an idiot's ride, complete with lunatic characters. The smooth and silken leg rolled into me, and the feel of it came through my jacket.

'Canals,' Elmo was saying. 'They got canals with houses on them, also a dock at the end where the water is good and deep.'

'Good idea, Elmo.'

'Wait'll you see.'

'How much further?'

'Maybe a half-hour now.'

'Listen — pull up somewhere, will you? I've got to see a man.'

239

'Haw!' said Elmo. 'Anywhere? No gas stations on this stretch.'

'Anywhere,' Toni said.

And what was her hand doing now? Tapping and touching my stomach, and then veering over to my right, where her skittering fingers slowed and stayed on my wrist. After that, I knew her purpose. She was handing me Masters' gun. She was slipping it into my open palm. Her fingers hesitated for a fraction of a second longer, and I thought I felt an extra pressure, the added weight of the little muscles in her hand squeezing mine.

Elmo swung off the main highway, slid around a turn, and brought the Caddy to a sudden stop on the crest of a small ridge. To the right, as the door swung open, I could see the remains of a brick wall, the crumbling stones left from a fire, because there was scattered debris around it. Toni stepped over me and got out. In another tick of my watch I would have to move, because Elmo was adjusting himself for a fresh cigarette at the wheel. I saw the flicker of his lighter and waited. I gave him a chance to take his first drag.

Then I got off my tail and hit him with the butt of Masters' gun. He went down, sagging against the door, and I was out of the car and yanking it open before he had a chance to recover. I hit him again and pulled him out. He was heavy as a sack of lead, and twice as cumbersome. I began to jerk his hulk of a body into the shadows near the wall. Toni stepped quickly my way from behind the white-washed bricks.

'You all right, Mike?'

I said, 'You're full of surprises.'

'He was going to kill you.'

'I didn't think you cared.'

'Mike . . . I didn't know about this . . . I . . . '

'Skip it. Find me some water — and fast.'

She ran back toward the yard, and I saw her fumbling around where a small stream whispered in the darkness. I leaned into Elmo and checked his breathing. I wanted him conscious again. I wanted him alive and vocal. Because he was going to tell me things.

Toni came back with a can full of water

and heaved it at him. He shook his head and blubbered a word, and then sank into never-never land again. I let him have the rest of it, and he blinked his eyes and groaned. He was grabbing at his head now. I slapped his hands away and jerked his head back against the concrete.

'Who sent you after me, Elmo?'

I showed him the automatic now. I put it where he couldn't miss it, under the broad curve of his fat nose. I pushed it into his face, letting him savor its smell and its flavor. He pulled his head back and moaned. But he said nothing.

'Who sent you, Elmo?'

He would be tough and stubborn. He was rallying now, releasing his big hands from his belt and leaning heavily on them, bobbing his head in the attitude of a Bowery drunk caught in a dark doorway. The sight of him pulled the string for me, reminding me of Izzy again, bringing it all back, complete with the blood and the torture in my partner's eyes. I was in no mood for cute games. I slapped Elmo across the jaw with the butt of the automatic. Hard.

'Who sent you, Elmo?'

How tough can you get? The head below me was mottled and pocked with blood, a splattered design brought on by the power of my last crack at him. He licked at his thick lips and shook his head, and said a few gurgled words to his inner man. His head was on a loose hinge and it was swaying slowly. He might go out if I let him. So I let him have more water. He came to life again and I grabbed his sweating head and slapped it back against the wall, enjoying the sound of it as it beat against the bricks. He fell forward heavily when I released him. He waved a weak and rubbery hand at me. I pulled him around and slapped him back and let him see the gun again. It was important now that he begin to talk. And fast.

'Who sent you, Elmo?'

And now his mouth opened and there was a gold glint in his uppers as he began to mumble, slack-jawed and slobbering.

'I'll talk,' he said.

'Talk.'

'Gilligan,' he said.

'You're working for him?'

'Gilligan,' he said again.

'How about Bruck?'

'No. Not Bruck.'

'Where is Gilligan?'

'Brentworth.'

'How long have you been with him?'

'Chicago,' said Elmo. 'Since Chicago.'

'Tell me more,' I said. 'Tell me about Linda Spain.'

'Who?' His head bobbed, and when he raised it, he hit the plaster behind him. 'Who?'

'Linda Spain, remember?'

I worked to refresh his memory, pushing the automatic into his jaw so that his eyes bulged at it and his breath came hard and rough again. He made a try at pushing himself through the wall. He failed.

I said, 'You were there, weren't you? You killed her?'

'I had to,' he gurgled. 'She . . . '

'That's enough. Then it was you who slugged me up there?'

'I had to . . . '

'Why?'

'Gilligan,' he said weakly.

'What's the deal?' I said. 'Why did Gilligan have to put her away?'

'I dunno.'

'And the fat man? You killed him, too?'

'No!' This time his voice rose on a new note. He was fighting to telegraph his sincerity. He shook his head violently. 'Not him!'

'You're a liar!'

'Not the fat guy,' Elmo whispered. 'I wasn't there.'

'Then who killed him?' I shouted.

'I dunno.'

'Did Gilligan do it?'

'I dunno.'

He was much too simple for histrionics, much too elemental for any play-acting. His eyes were sick with fear, riveted on the gun with an intensity that almost made them pop out of his head. He was leveling.

'And Gilligan sent you to the apartment to mess up Izzy Rosen?'

'Who?'

'The little guy.'

'Oh, him. I didn't mean to hurt him bad . . . '

That was the payoff for me. I kicked up at him, high on the head this time, where he had hit Izzy. All my pent-up fury went into the kick: my toe caught the rim of his jaw and the sound of the leather was a flat clop and the blood came oozing out of the crimson welt. The heat of my anger held me there, watching him sag and roll over, his hairy hands clutching at some invisible support. But he grabbed nothing at all.

And then he slid over in the dirt and lay still.

27

Southern State Parkway — Long Island
12:21 A.M. — July 20th

I wheeled the Caddy back on the highway
and headed for New York. It was getting
late and there were things to do
— important things. Toni sat away from
me, saying nothing. Words would be
useless now, because she had already told
me where she stood on Gilligan's list. She
was no part of the murder and mayhem
routine. He had assigned her to me as a
watchdog, but his fancy poodle had let
him down. He would be surprised, could
he see her now, her deep eyes riveted on
some personal vista far ahead of us. Once
she half-turned to me, and I saw her
mouth open tentatively, but she bit her lip
and preserved her silence. And from then
on in, I devoted my mental hijinks to
Gilligan. He would be sitting in a soft seat
now, quietly licking his lean chops over

his past performance in the game of hide-and-seek we were playing. I yearned to start for the Brentworth at once, to let him feel the same toe that had mashed Elmo's jaw. But there were things to do.

I raced off the Manhattan Bridge and swung uptown, parking before the drugstore on the corner of Wragge's block.

I said, 'Inside, Toni. I may need you.'

She followed without a word. The pimply clerk grinned at me from behind the counter, his mouth open in a fly-chasing pose. He leaned my way and extended a palm and gave me his smug and priggish smile, complete with a whinnying laugh he must have learned at the Belmont track.

'Pay me,' he wheezed.

'For what?'

'Lady Lombar, mister.'

'She came in?'

'What kind of a bookie are you? She ran five lengths ahead of the favorite, Gertrude Gong.'

'I missed her, I guess.'

'So now you know,' said the clerk. 'So now you pay off, mister — eleven-thirty.'

He pocketed the money eagerly. He was now a changed character — light and breezy and full of fun. He offered Toni a drink. He offered me a drink. Nothing warms a horse player to intimacy quicker than a few bucks back from the bookie. He began to reel off a list of bets for tomorrow. I took them on and let him chatter. Then I grabbed one of his menus and took out my broken sketching pencil and began to draw. My head bounced and burned from the massage Elmo had twice given me. There was a clattering behind my ears, a combination of dull pain and burning anxiety, a double dose of dizziness that did not make my job easy. I asked the clerk for a couple of aspirins and downed them fast, then returned to my job, conscious of Toni's eyes following my pencil as it eked out the contours of Wragge's face. After a while, the pain dulled and I was able to concentrate.

I fought to recreate the picture of Wragge — my last sight of him, just before I fell into the heavy sleep of exhaustion in my compartment on the train. I doodled a square. This was the basic shape of his head, an almost perfect square. I tried him in full-face, sketching his massive brows and working for some clue as to the important symbols of his personality.

' . . . and then this nag, Bernie Hanover, starts around the backstretch,' the clerk was saying.

I barely heard him. I was deep in my personal creative trance, the sweaty moment when inspiration comes to the amateur caricaturist. Then the little nerves behind the ears set up a screaming, a shouting that bubbles through the ego and sifts slowly past the filter of the selective brain. I began to see Sidney Wragge clearly, his huge head outlined against the black window of the train, his features frozen in a stolid pose. He was coming through to me. I began with his eyebrows, shaggy and uncombed. This was the key to his caricature, for the sleepy eyes lay buried in soft, deep pockets beneath those brows. And after the eyebrows I recalled the nose, a small and sharp classic beak, complete with flared nostrils that added a note of animal keenness to his larded face. I rubbed in the shadows and blackened my outline. Now the profile shot was finished.

The clerk had stopped gabbling about Roosevelt Raceway. He stared at my finished sketches with the curious eye of a critic, awed by my quick skill with the pencil, yet troubled by the pictures I had drawn.

'You draw real good,' he said.

'Do I? You recognize this character?'

'I dunno.'

He lifted the paper and adjusted it under his nose. He stared and squinted at it. He rubbed his chin and scratched at an annoying itch somewhere deep under his mat of hair. He jerked his head backward and forward, assumed a critical air, registered recognition and befuddlement, satisfaction and disappointment, as fussy as a connoisseur over a faked masterpiece.

'I dunno,' he said again.

'What don't you know?'

'Is it supposed to be Sidney?'

'Doesn't it look like him?'

'A little bit, here, where you got him front view.' He paused and shook his head again. 'But the side view, now — that's not Sidney at all.'

I handed the sketches to Toni. She said, 'He's wrong, Mike. You caught him the way I remember him.' She shivered a little. 'Especially the profile shot.'

'Are you kidding?' asked the clerk. 'That ain't Sidney at all.'

'Why isn't it Sidney?' I asked.

'The nose, mostly.'

'What's wrong with the nose?'

'Sidney didn't have such a sharp nose.'

'Are you sure?'

'I'm not only sure now,' he said, 'but I am also positive. You know why? Because it just so happens Sidney comes in here for nose drops all the time. A post-nasal drip, he has, I guess. So naturally, when a man talks about his schnozzle so much — why, you sort of get to know it. You sort of pay extra attention, if you get what I mean.' He made a sour face at the head-on view of Wragge, my first sketch of him. 'What threw me off was this here picture, see? Because, from the front, Sidney could be any other type of fat man; Hoover, maybe, when he was younger. Or Fatty Arbuckle. Fat guys are hard to draw from the front, is that it?'

'Tough as hell,' I admitted. 'But you still think my profile shot of him is way off?'

'It just ain't Sidney, is all. Not that nose. Sidney also don't look so mean.'

'I guess you're right. Sidney's the jolly fat boy type, right?'

'Exactly. A regular guy.'

'Sure. The best in the world.'

'Right. I never met a guy in the bookie business exactly like Sid. Always a happy smile, even on a big payoff. Like the time I had that longshot at Aqueduct . . . '

His voice faded off, lost to me now, as meaningless as the sighing of a distant wind, or the noise of the city outside. My mind was on fire. I had planted the seeds by myself, and now the fruit was ripe, the enigma solved for me. The recent past rose up to dig at my racing corpuscles: the beginning of it, all the way back to Chicago and Rico Bruck and Gilligan and the assignment; all the way through the trip to New York, complete with the fat and ominous hulk of Sidney Wragge, his larded face crushed to a bloody pulp in my room at the Brentworth. The route was polished with the crimson stain of murder, a mad and frantic chase through the city, in search of everything and nothing. And now I had the answer. I stared beyond the clerk's shoulder, through the wall, and beyond the wall to the next stop on the trolley line to death. Something of my purpose must have come through to Toni, because she grabbed my arm and held tight, and wouldn't let go when I tried to shake her off.

I turned to face her. 'Let's get out of here,' I said, pulling her off the stool and into the street. 'We've got a little chore to do.'

I hesitated in the shadow of a sleeping building, jerking her close to me, so close that I could see the softness in her eyes.

I said, 'I need your help, Toni.'

'What do you want me to do?'

'You've got to go down to the police.'

'The police?' She trembled, on fire with worry. 'I don't get you, Mike.'

'I'll need them at the Brentworth Hotel

— in about thirty minutes.'

'And you're willing to trust me?' she asked. 'I could run out on you.'

'You could, but you won't,' I said.

We were in the doorway to an apartment house, back in the shadows, deep in the quiet. The light from across the street filtered in, and lit her face with a strange and subtle glow. Her eyes were steady on mine. She was adding me up again. She was staring at me with an intensity that would have rocked me and ruined me at any other time but this. Right now I needed her, and she knew it, and she was working to prove that she merited my trust. She put a cold hand on my wrist. She came closer to me and began to talk.

'I'm glad you feel that way about me, Mike. Because I wouldn't want you to think of me any other way. I wouldn't want you to think that I knew what Elmo was going to do to your partner.'

'Skip it,' I said.

She was close enough so that I could feel the intimate shape of her against my chest, and hear the sound of her breathing, and smell the sweetness of her breath. And then something happened to her and she went soft again and melted against me and wiped her eyes.

And she was whispering when she said, 'Tell me exactly what you want done, Mike. I promise to do it.'

So I told her.

28

The street was a black canyon, a gloomy alley, a corridor of quiet. The scene was no tonic for my frayed sensibilities. I was counting on Toni to skip back to the police. I was depending on her to give them my message, to have the squad cars around the Brentworth in about twenty-five minutes.

Would she do it? The memory of my last moment with her revived my confidence. But after that, other memories rose up to dim my hopes. Anger prickled my scalp and heated the back of my neck. I thought vaguely of what I would do if she didn't come through for me. But the upsurge of emotion died quickly in me. The Brentworth challenged me from across the street. I stepped out of the shadows and headed for the entrance.

The canopy shed a weak light on the pavement, yellowish and soupy. In the lobby, the light seemed paler and dusty; as old as the hotel itself. Two small lamps glowed among the empty chairs, and there were no guests lounging under the potted palms. From somewhere behind me, a radio blared the muted strains of a late-hour disc jockey show. Ahead of me a clerk dozed behind the desk, leaning on an elbow and snoring with abandon. I approached him and coughed politely.

He didn't respond. So I knocked his elbow off the register.

'Yes?' He eyed me with the approval of a Tiffany clerk who finds a dead herring on his counter.

'Mr. Gilligan,' I said.

'Not in.'

'Really? I had an appointment with him.'

'Not in,' he said again, brushing an imaginary fleck of dandruff off his lapel.

'Do you mind phoning him?' I asked.

'I do, indeed.'

'Do you mind telling me his room number?'

'Ask Mr. Gilligan.'

But I didn't have time for asking Mr. Gilligan. So I reached over and grabbed him, high and tight on his blue serge. I pulled him my way so that he hung over the desk. Then I said, 'I'm asking you *pretty please* — Gilligan's room number?'

'Go to hell.'

There would be nothing in it for him, nothing but a short and pleasant coma, because the elevators were around the abutment in the lobby, and nobody could hear me as I went to work on him. He had a wide and pimpled head, and a manner that irritated me, because every second was important to me. So I caught him by his tie and turned it like a crank, twisting it until he clawed out at me, the breath coming hard and rasping from his mouth. I put a fist in his navel and his tongue dropped a bit, then the sweat came and he began to cough and splutter.

'Nine-oh-five,' he gasped.

'Good boy.'

I didn't want him around to bother me anymore. I yanked him again and his head jerked forward, within hitting distance. And then I hit him, not hard, but in the right spot, a stiff crack that caught him on the point of his receding jaw. He sagged and fell at me; I caught him and dropped him behind the counter and on the floor, where he belonged.

He would be dreaming for a long time. The ninth floor was a kick in the mental pants for me. How many hours ago had I been there? I walked slowly down the crimson carpet and stood near the door to 904, where it had all begun. A few feet beyond that door, on the same wall, was the number 905, and the sight of it brought a strange surge of laughter to my lips: quiet laughter, the feeble edge of my frustration. The little gears in my mental machine clicked disturbingly, taking me back to the first few heated hours with Toni Kaye, reminding me that all this had happened very close to Room 905. And was Gilligan sitting behind the wall in his suite, enjoying my antics, smiling with satisfaction at the role he had created for me? And what was Gilligan doing now?

I advanced to his door and put my ear

against it. There was the sound of speech in there, dull and muffled. The voices were low-pitched and muted. A glass tinkled vaguely. A drinking party? And then somebody laughed, and the laughter beat against the inner wall of my brain and tightened me where I stood, because the laughter was not Gilligan's. It was a weird laugh, a zany laugh, a chuckle compounded of depth and personality, an impossible burst of amusement that seemed to come from out of the recent past. And the laughter moved me to action.

I opened the door and walked in.

And then I froze.

John Gilligan stood at the window, his head turned my way, an expression of complete and uncontrolled bewilderment popping his eyes. But Gilligan didn't hold me for more than a tick of time. I was looking to his right, at the man who sat in the big red leather chair, facing me. The sight of him made me swallow hard. My throat seemed suddenly sanded and dry, and all my muscles went quickly tight. Because of his monstrous bulk. Because he sat there staring at me, his heavy brows lowered over the deep and saturnine pits of his eyes. In the split second of my entry, his larded visage hardened in a mask of officious anger, a pose that I remembered well. Because the man in the red leather chair was Sidney Wragge!

And, since he was Sidney Wragge, he opened his slit of a mouth and spoke.

'Mr. Wells,' he said with his usual show of dignity. 'This is a surprise.'

There was not time for hauling out my automatic. Gilligan came alive at the window, his face empty of its accustomed collegiate ease, his lean frame alert and almost athletic in its movement. He had a gun in his hands out of nowhere, and he was stepping forward and waving it at me, in the way that a small boy converts himself into a Western hero. He was Hopalong Cassidy without his nag. He was the big bad menace, complete with all the sliding gestures that make up the act. But there was nothing amateurish in the way he dug the nose of his armament into my gut and pushed me back and against the wall. His hands were on me and all over me in a quick flash of energy, and he was yanking out my automatic and shoving it away before I could call him a dirty name.

'Who let you in, Wells?' he asked.

'You don't train your front office well,' I said. 'The guy at the desk was easy.'

'Mr. Wells is the muscular type,' said Wragge, chuckling at me with a brief surge of humor. He did not hold the pose. His great and shaggy brows came down in a frown that was meant to wilt any starch left in my sweating collar. 'Mr. Wells is also the clever type,' he added. 'How did you guess that I'd be here, Mr. Wells?'

I said, 'You can blame your friend Gilligan.'

'Gilligan?' Wragge asked his fingertips. 'How?'

'Tell your partner, Gilligan,' I said.

'Partner?' Wragge asked. He was as cool as a Tom Collins spiked with arsenic. He continued to hold a little monologue with his pudgy fingers. 'Mr. Wells is a clever man, John. You see, he knows everything. It's unfortunate, however, that this is the wrong moment for knowing so much, Wells. Sometimes a man can dig his own grave with his loose tongue.'

He was telling me! I stood there looking at both of them, feeling the beat of my heart up high somewhere near my throat. Minutes were passing, and it was important that I keep the clock ticking away. Gilligan snaked his eyes at Wragge, and there was a hint of blossoming fright in the exchange. He was the bottom boy in the deal. He was the junior assistant, the fall guy, the henchman in this scene. Wragge surveyed him with the same tolerant air he used when talking to me. And Gilligan didn't care for the role. Gilligan was in no mood for any more idle conversation. Something had happened to his courtroom manner. He had left it somewhere back in Chicago, where he had left his reputation to gamble with Sidney Wragge. Instead of his usual slick and calm deportment, Gilligan seemed wired for sound, a loudspeaker who would talk only when Wragge pressed the button. Gilligan was twitchy. He held his gun with a nervousness that scared me more than the look on the fat man's face. Gilligan might tremble too much and pull the trigger and make the place noisy. Wragge saw his mental upheaval and didn't like it.

'Put your gun away, John,' said Wragge. 'I'll take care of Mr. Wells.'

'My pleasure,' said Gilligan. He tried to laugh, but produced only a high and off-key cackle. 'Let's hear it, Wells, all the way'

'This is no courtroom,' I said. It pleased me to see him go red and flustered. He wanted to be the big bad man. He wanted to justify his manhood for Wragge, to prove himself, to show that he was hard and mean. But all he could raise was an angry flood of blood pressure, as weak and meaningless as a blushing virgin. 'What the hell do you think you are, Gilligan — Mr. District Attorney?'

So he hit me. The right cross he delivered was better than I thought he could manage. He clipped me across the jaw and I went down, upsetting a small table behind me. Gilligan pulled me up and made me sit, and goosed me with the automatic. It was all very jolly. I was gaining time, but it would cost me all my teeth for the long delay I needed.

'Now, then,' said Gilligan, borrowing a bit from Wragge's book of poise, 'let's have it, Wells.'

'What?'

'How did you manage to guess what was going on?'

'Toni Kaye,' I said.

'You're lying!'

Beyond Gilligan's right arm, my eyes caught the figure of Sidney Wragge, bending forward in the easy chair now, caught up in the first shock of my little narrative. I had pricked him where it meant something.

'Toni Kaye knew nothing,' said Wragge.

'Of course she knew nothing,' I said. 'But you made your biggest mistake when you hired her. You thought she'd soften me up — and you were right, Gilligan. She could soften up anything on legs except chairs and tables. She's good. She's terrific. But you didn't trust her, did you? You should have let her be, once she arrived in New York. Instead, you decided to visit her. Toni's a bad housekeeper, Gilligan. But all of a sudden, she began to go cute on me. I caught her cleaning ashtrays. That was a funny little bit, believe me. It put me in the role of a television detective. It made me look around for crumbs. And I found them, Gilligan. You forgot to leave your stinking little pipe home when you went to call on her. She couldn't get those crumbs out of the place quick enough. Is that a laugh?'

Gilligan didn't find it amusing. Something was happening to Wragge in the pause. The fat man was shaking his massive head at his junior partner. The fat man was bubbling with anger.

'Where is she?' Wragge asked.

'At a place called the Rivington,' Gilligan said.

'Send Elmo over for her.'

'You can't do that, can you?' I asked Gilligan. 'Tell Mr. Wragge why, Junior.'

'Why can't you do it?' Wragge snapped.

Gilligan squirmed and said nothing.

I said, 'Because Gilligan sent Elmo out to put *me* away. Didn't you, Junior?'

Gilligan sucked more air, avoiding the eyes of his partner.

'Elmo did his best,' I said. 'But it wasn't good enough. You'll find him out on Long Island, but you won't find him in one piece. Sending the gorilla out to butcher me was a dandy idea — but you thought of it too late. He hit me when I was just finishing with the other fat man's apartment, when I was searching for the crumb of information Izzy Rosen found — in the refrigerator.'

'And what was that, Wells?' Wragge asked.

'You messed up there, Wragge. You're much too well-bred to be gnawing stale veal cutlets and drinking cheap soda pop. And why should you save bacon drippings? When you set up the double you intended to kill, you should have sent him to finishing school for a while until he learned your personal habits. You should have schooled him in the gentle art of mattress bouncing, too.'

'Mr. Wells is cleverer than I imagined,' Wragge commented.

'How dumb can a private dick get?' I

asked. 'You practically threw things at me when you forgot to eliminate Linda Spain before I met her. Linda was a cheap bump-and-grind queen, Wragge. The other fat man might have cared for her, but you wouldn't give that type a passing nod. Linda was cheap, and so was the man who made love to her. He bought her a corny chromo and an incense burner out of an uptown dump. I checked that picture, Wragge. And when I began my research, it seemed funny as hell to me that a man of your taste could ever buy a chromo of that sort. I'd figure you more the modern, progressive art fancier. You'd rather buy a Picasso reproduction than the mangy daub your double got for Linda. The picture in her living room didn't match your personality, Wragge.

'The man you hired to die for you was too lowbrow, all the way. He took horse bets and ate garbage and made love like one of the common people. You should have taken all that into consideration when you set him up to be butchered in your place. You had a perfect scheme for fooling the police about him. You had a terrific gimmick for sucking in Rico Bruck and Monk Stang. Each would believe the other had the Folsom pendant, so long as the police didn't recover it. In the meantime, your double would die for you . . . and you'd be free to cash in on the gems and spend the profits with your Boy Scout friend Gilligan.'

'A masterpiece of deduction,' breathed Wragge, his eyes closed, his fingers tapping the edge of his chair in a slow and deliberate rhythm.

'Isn't it dandy?' I asked Gilligan. 'I can't wait to see Rico Bruck's face when he finds out about this.'

'That is a sight you will never enjoy,' Wragge said. 'Because Gilligan and I do not choose to have Bruck find out about this.'

Wragge sighed mournfully and raised his ponderous bulk in the chair. Time! I needed more time for these two. The minutes had flown. I wondered whether Toni had reached the police yet, and how they were reacting to her message, and whether they would be sending the squad cars up here. And when?

270

Standing, Wragge loomed larger than I remembered him; but this might have been an optical trick, because he wore a different suit now: a gray, double-breasted item that had been well-tailored to his massive figure. He picked up his gray hat and surveyed me wearily, fixing me with his tight-lipped smile.

'We shall have to use the roof, John,' he said. 'Come along, Wells.'

29

Gilligan led the parade through the hall and out to the fire exit and up the stairs to the roof. Behind me, I felt the metal nose of Wragge's automatic. His hand did not quiver as he pushed it hard against me, digging it into the flesh around my kidneys, prodding me with every step, to remind me that he would never leave me, not until he had left me stiff somewhere. His breath wheezed huskily in the silence, telling me of the strain of his climb on his larded frame. Our footsteps clattered and echoed up the stairwell, beating a dull but deliberate rhythm as we went higher and higher. We would be up there soon, and they would be taking me across the roof to another building. Wragge must have planned this exit a long time ago, in case of any emergency of this kind. There would be a car waiting on the next block, and he and Gilligan would escort me to a convenient spot for mayhem. They would be thorough about me. These were intelligences, two brains who would not be sidetracked from their purpose. They would wrap me up and bounce me into eternity.

And then we were stepping through the door to the roof. A breath of cool air hit me, but it reached no deeper than the edge of my sweating face. Inside me, a panic was building, the dry-throated clawing of fear that I was on my way to sudden death. I was stepping into the clammy darkness atop the Brentworth, and the night was whispering to me, telling me that Toni Kaye would never come, that this was the end of the line for me.

I thought of her in a rush of remembrance, all the way back to the sunlit entrance of the Card Club where she had made her first pitch for me, the prearranged come-on that was meant to lure me into the game Gilligan had devised. I thought of her with mixed emotions, cursing her for her luscious body and her teasing face. Had she changed at all during the last two days? What had happened to her on the road out to Long Island? What had stirred her to act for me? My mind was bright with the last vivid picture of her, the last quick moment before I headed this way. She had looked into my eyes and told me that I could depend on her.

She had sold me a bill of goods.

And as the door to the roof squealed shut behind me, I realized that I was whistling in the dark. Toni Kaye had probably headed out of town.

'To the left, Wells.'

Wragge's voice had lost some of its measured softness. He pushed me where he wanted me, across the roof and behind an abutment, and under a few stray wires left over from the era of radio aerials. Ahead of me, the roof ended. There was a slight rise to the side that faced the alley. Beyond, over the dim ridge of the silhouetted buildings, a vague crimson mist hung over the area above Times Square. The Paramount clock stood at

2:03. In all the fogged vista ahead of me, not one light burned, not one office building glowed with life. The sounds of the city seemed to come from over the hills and far away — the occasional bark of a taxi horn, the distant hiss of tires, a voice, a laugh. And silence. Would they dare shoot a gun in this void? The noise of it would go screaming through the streets, rousing the guests in the hotel below. A gun would be simple and direct, but it would lack subtlety.

'Keep walking, Wells.'

Where did he want me to walk? A few yards ahead lay the edge of the roof. The nauseating knowledge of Wragge's purpose rose up to make me gasp in horror.

'What's the gimmick?' I asked again, aware of the answer before it would leave his lips. Time! I needed every second, every precious ticking instant, every breath, every pause, every possible delay.

'Keep walking,' said Wragge.

'Over the edge?'

'Would you rather be pushed?'

'I'm not the suicidal type,' I said.

'Push him, John,' said the fat man.

One step! Gilligan was taking it, toward me, the sound of it clear and sharp in the sticky silence. A footfall. A flick of time, an instant, a chip of a second, a breath, a sigh, a heartbeat. And what would I do with the moment? How could I use it? It was a time for clear thinking, a time to be the wise guy, the sage and smart detective. Instead, nothing but sweaty terror boiled in my brain. My ears were burning with pressure, listening for the sound of a siren, the noise of the squad cars on their way to rescue me, like the Marines in a grade-D Hollywood opera. But nothing rose out of the vastness of the surrounding city, no unusual sound except the hammering of the blood in my ears.

Another step! Gilligan was closer and only a breath of living had elapsed. My eyes searched the rooftop for something to use — an old pipe, a rotted aerial pole, a convenient brick. But somebody had cleaned this roof not too long ago. It was as barren as an empty tabletop.

Until I saw the ladder on my left! There was hope in that ladder, a small out; a chance if I could work it in time. Down below, the fire escape led to the alley. If I could make the ladder, what then? But Gilligan was taking still another step, and now he was behind me, and the big moment had come.

I lunged back at him. I caught him squarely in the gut, and his gun went off. The flat clap of thunder from its muzzle screamed into the still night. I was hit.

A stab of pain shot through my shoulder, and my right arm felt as useless as a broken crutch. Gilligan had fallen back under my sudden lunge. But now he was alive again, and coming after me fast. I crawled toward the ladder and hung on. I dropped myself over the edge, and when my hands grabbed the siding somebody stood over me and kicked out at me with sudden ferocity. It was Gilligan again. He was doing his damnedest to kick me off the edge of the ladder and down into the black hole of the alley. I heard Wragge mutter a sharp and deep-throated command as I dropped one step lower on the ladder and fought to keep my right arm from falling off my burning shoulder.

Gilligan hit down at me with his gun butt. He caught me on the other side this time, and I grabbed for his arm and made it. I yanked him my way. He was surprisingly tough to move. But anger and pain had made me a madman. I pulled hard at him, and he slipped toward the edge of the roof, kicking for my head and wheezing strangely, like a frightened animal or a frustrated boy in a schoolyard brawl. I caught his shoe and held on. I yanked and jerked. And then, howling and screaming, Gilligan slipped toward me, and over me and off the roof, falling and yammering his terror to the skittering wind. He went down yowling all the way until a final thud ended his trip to hell.

I lifted my head cautiously above the line of the roof. Where was Wragge? Hot fury dimmed my eyes and forced me to take a zany chance. I forgot about everything but Wragge. I remembered his cool and murderous sagacity. He would be waiting for me in a dark corner, somewhere where I least expected him. He would be standing quietly by, letting me grope and stumble until he could level me with one powerful sweep of his giant arm. I flattened myself on the rooftop and looked around.

Silence. If he was here, he was anchored. He was already in position to strike his lethal blow. The deck was stacked his way now. If he could get rid of me, his little game would be over. And then the sweat began to crawl over me. And then my gut began to burn with a fresh and mounting nausea. Wragge *must* get rid of me! He had set the stage perfectly for the end of the melodrama, the last quick scene before curtain time.

I realized, suddenly, that Gilligan had been almost too easy to pull over the edge of the roof. I knew now that Wragge had helped me pull him over!

And when the knowledge hit me, my eyes went dry and my breath came hot and rasping. I searched the dim corners of the rooftop for the spot where Wragge had chosen to hide his larded body. I rolled slowly to the right, keeping in the clear. The door lay ahead, and beyond the door, the dim edge of the adjoining building. Wragge would be somewhere in between, waiting for me to cross the roof toward the exit.

I got to my knees and began to crawl slowly toward the abutment between me and the door. He must be behind there! I groped and clutched at the slick surface of the roof, feeling for everything and anything. And then I found it — a broken aerial post, about two feet of metal and heavy enough for manslaughter. I went forward again and reached the corner of the abutment and dove blindly into the dimness beyond.

Then all hell broke loose. Wragge caught the full strength of my attack and came back at me with a violence that knocked the wind out of me.

I brought up the metal rod and beat out at him blindly. He was a mountain of brute power, an elephant toying with a mouse. He fell back a step and hit me behind the ear, then dropped me to the roof again. I clung to his beefy legs and pushed. My right arm was now worthless. I had only one chance: a quick shot at his stomach with the rod. But he must have sensed the urgency in my maneuver.

Because he sidestepped me and aimed a kick at my face, as agile as an athlete, as quick as a fox. His foot skimmed my jaw and now he was off balance; I caught his leg and jerked hard, and heard him mutter a bad word at me as he fell over on his back, a carload of meat, puffing and blowing as he tumbled. Then I went at him. The metal rod was lost to me, but I hammered at his paunch with my fist. Was he laughing at me? Where was the bastard rolling now? He dragged me with him as he righted himself; I struggled to grab him, but he was slipping away and bringing his hands down to my throat. He squeezed. I kicked out at him: my toe caught his midsection and forced an animal grunt from him. But I was on the way out now, and he knew it.

From somewhere in a distant province, the sound of a screaming siren flooded the air. Closer? Or was it the mad screaming of my angry hate that whistled in my ears. Up? Was he lifting me now? I bit out at his arm and felt the soft flesh of his wrist in my mouth. I bit harder, and he trembled and paused, lowered me, and shouted a deep-throated obscenity at me. The sirens were bright sharp stabs of hysteria now, echoing in my ears. Wragge reached down for me again, and the last thing I saw was the gray, shapeless lump of his tremendous body, and the last thing I heard was the sound of a thousand horses galloping across the tarred roof. And a shout of pain when the world exploded in my face.

After that, I dropped into oblivion.

30

Time was a vague and shapeless thing. I drifted on a large and grayish cloud, high above the city, so high that the earth seemed lost below. There were countless floating things up at this level with me, but everything whirled and swayed and drifted without purpose. There was a girl on a small cloud who passed my way and winked at me, but when I grabbed out for her, my anxious hands caught nothing but the wind. So I sat and waited on my personal nimbus and after a while the earth loomed larger, a billiard ball, a beach ball, and finally a rushing, looming thing that would catch me soon, because I had fallen off my cloud and was descending rapidly. I was headed down now, chasing the girl on the tiny cloud. She fell at a whistling clip, and I grabbed

283

for her silken shanks and held on. Then we sailed through the fog and into the realm of living, and we were hurtling through the last thin edge of space and headed for a crash. Somebody screamed at us, and there was silence and I knew that nothing could stop us now. I dropped to earth with a gasping groan.

And then somebody was shaking me.

And a cool hand held mine.

And a cool voice said, 'How do you feel, Mr. Wells?'

The room was white and the air was white, and the light was white and her figure was white; a white voice from a white face with a white hat perched on white hair. I rubbed my eyes with my good hand, because the other one was bedded down in a stiff and awkward cast. Somebody had wrapped my head in bandages, and the man who sat at the side of the bed was bundled in the same way. He leaned toward me, and I gawked at him and laughed when his misted shape came through to me.

'Izzy,' I said. 'It's a small world.'

'You mustn't talk too much,' the nurse

said. She was suddenly familiar, the little doll I had met here before. She was Magda Prionee, pretty enough to be featured on *Life*'s cover.

'How long have I been here?' I asked.

'Almost two days,' Magda said. 'You were badly hurt, Mr. Wells.'

'But you should have seen the other guy,' Izzy laughed. 'You sure put a dent in the fat man, Mike. Leach says you almost bit his wrist off.'

'Did Leach find the Folsom cluster?'

'Wragge had it on him. Leach caught him trying to leave by way of the next building. He would have made it, too, only the door was jammed a bit, and Wragge couldn't open it fast enough with his left hand. You bit hard enough to put his right hand out of commission. He made a mistake when he tried to shoot his way off the roof with Leach's boys. He didn't know that they were all over the place, including the next building. He was shot twice, Leach says, and the second slug killed him.'

'I'm feeling no pain.' I smiled. Izzy lit a cigarette for me, and I puffed it hungrily and let the room come into focus. Magda stood close to Izzy, smiling down at me. She had a round and girlish face; a blue-eyed doll with a high tan, and the whitest teeth this side of the toothpaste ads. She took my pulse; her fingers felt soft and tender, and their pressure was making my blood bounce and gurgle in its normal tempo. She had dark hair and a good figure. I thought of Toni right away.

'What did Leach say about the girl, Izzy?'

'What girl?'

'Toni Kaye. She came through for me. I owe her something.'

'Oh, that one.' Izzy laughed. 'She came up to see you after they brought you in, Mike. She had a message for you. She told me to tell you that she was going back to Chicago. She didn't like it here in New York. Said the town was too fast for her. Said you'd understand. Funny thing — I could have sworn the doll was crying when she left the hospital. You and she had something special cooking?'

'A pretty good stew,' I said. 'But maybe

a bit too highly flavored for anything but indigestion.'

'Double talk,' said Izzy. 'Did she help you?'

'In a roundabout way. But she almost arranged for your funeral, chum. She didn't mean it, I'm sure, but Elmo almost bumped you off because of Toni. What did you have down at the apartment? What did you find that you wanted me to see? The refrigerator?'

'Of course the refrigerator. The way you described Wragge to me, he couldn't possibly have eaten the trash in that icebox. Right?'

We talked about it. We went back over it and chewed the small pieces and enjoyed the crumbs, because it was all over now and we could afford the luxury of it, like two gourmets licking their chops over a tasty meal. It was down, swallowed, and lived through. It was a finished feast, and we were burping our delight now that the moment had arrived for the demi-tasse and brandy. And when we had finished with the tasty bits, Magda stepped forward and tapped Izzy on the shoulder delicately, reminding both of us that we were semi-invalids.

She led him to the door, and he waved a hand at me and was gone. Then Magda busied herself at the window, adjusting the Venetian blinds. The light was strong out there. The sun streamed in and lit the outline of her supple figure, so that the rounded contours of it were a gray shape under the starched uniform. In that pose, she lingered at the window until the shades were adjusted just so and the room was bathed in a quiet gloom. Magda sat down near the bed and crossed her legs; even with the big white hospital brogans on, she had knees worthy of a chorus line. She got me a glass of water, and her figure moved gracefully as she reached for it on the small end table. I let her feed me the water and her cheeks went hot when I grabbed her free hand. There was something burning in her eyes, and I wondered vaguely how long it would take me to find out what it was; and, if it was what I thought it was, how much longer after that to share her personal fire.

'You've been awfully nice to Izzy,' I said.

'Just my job,' said Magda.

'You're modest, Magda. Izzy told me you were extra nice to him. He thinks you're the prettiest nurse in the hospital.'

'He hasn't seen them all.'

'You don't know Izzy. He gets around.'

She smiled at that one, and didn't pull her hand away. When she blushed her face lit with color, like a farm girl just after heaving the hay. I began to ask myself questions about her. And all the time I squeezed her hand and made sly verbal passes at her. After a while she began to return the pressure.

'I shouldn't be here so long,' she said. 'You must have your rest, if you ever want to get out of here.'

'Maybe I'd rather stay.'

'Don't say that. The doctor doesn't want any complications.'

'To hell with the doctor,' I said. 'Don't move away, or I'll go into a coma.'

She didn't move. She couldn't. I held her with my left hand, but I was always a switch hitter back in school. And pretty soon she stopped blushing and laughed at my jokes.

When that happened, I began to feel normal again.